C000304164

HIDDEN IN THE HEART

HIDDEN IN THE HEART

DAN JACOBSON

BLOOMSBURY

First published 1991
Copyright © 1991 by Dan Jacobson
The moral right of the author has been asserted.
Bloomsbury Publishing Ltd, 2 Soho Square, London W1V 5DE

A CIP catalogue record for this book
is available from the British Library

ISBN 0 7475 0981 6

10 9 8 7 6 5 4 3 2 1

Typeset by Hewer Text Composition Services, Edinburgh
Printed and bound in Great Britain by
Butler & Tanner Limited, Frome and London

O what is hidden in the heart of her
that I have still to learn?

Adrian Bester: 'Song'

PART ONE

PART ONE

ONE

Yesterday – no, the day before – I read in the paper that Rodney Foxborough had at last died.

That is what has brought me here, staring into this screen: writing, after a fashion.

The way he hung on! People who drink a lot are supposed to be a bad risk, actuarially speaking. But not Foxborough. He drank and he drank, and he lived and he lived. I had almost begun to take it for granted that he would outlive me: the more than forty years' advantage I supposedly had over him, in that respect, hardly seemed to matter at all.

Diana Foxborough was duly mentioned in the obituary, of course, with her maiden name in brackets. Ditto with his first wife. Then the one he is 'survived by'. And the names of his three sons. He had one by each marriage, apparently. The symmetry of the arrangement must have pleased the poet's heart. A matching of content to form, as it were.

Anyhow, now that he has gone, the last of them to go, I am free, if I so wish, to tell everyone all I know about Foxborough and Diana and her one-time lover: the man who was later to become my lover too, my confidant and friend.

He once told me, this friend of mine, that when he was in Diana's company he had the feeling that he was running a race against her; a race which he could not win and she could only lose. So obsessed was he with the eighteen years she was ahead of him, in that fatal race! Then she died; and later he died, too; and more years passed; more than ten, more than twenty, after Diana's death; and behold Rodney Foxborough, the immortal, married yet once more, still walking the earth, like some kind of Struldbrug, one of those creatures in *Gulliver's Travels* who never die.

And me, here, forgotten, unforgetting.

Long after Diana's death I was told too by her former lover (and mine) that he sometimes felt as if nothing would be easier for him than to step back into the time and space they occupied then . . . and do everything all over again. But differently. It seemed to him, he said, that the selves they used to be were still standing there, exactly as they once did, waiting patiently for his return.

He also said that in his dreams he and Diana would occasionally find themselves together. They would meet in the simplest, most matter-of-fact fashion. Only, her face was always averted from him. Even when he reached out to embrace her, and she gave herself to him, her face was turned away. 'You're still punishing me!' he wanted to cry out. She said nothing; and when he woke he knew that all he had done was to use her to punish himself.

As before. As always.

*

If I wanted to, I could add something to the annals of English literature that will otherwise remain forever unknown. Not a poem by Rodney Foxborough, God forbid, but an item of biographical information about him which has failed to appear in the obituaries. (Yes, when I heard that he had died I did go out and buy all the papers which I thought might carry an obituary of him. Anyone who had seen me at the newsagent's, picking up this newspaper and that, could well have supposed me to be some anxious, ambitious wretch who has just had a book come out, or a play produced, and now goes rushing to get hold of the reviews.)

These reviews – I beg your pardon: these obituaries – speak of him as poet, wartime code-breaker, critic, jester, old Westminster, BBC man, raconteur, eccentric etc.; they even refer to him, in discreet but jocular fashion, as a drinker. What they leave out, what everyone will leave out in their accounts of him – unless I spill the beans – is that the man was also a murderer.

*

All I have to do is to push (twice) the oddly shaped switch sitting at the bottom left of the screen in front of me, thus

4

ignoring the warning that will momentarily appear on it (HAVE YOU TRANSFERRED TO DISK?). Instantly I will have become a non-writer again. A tiny flash of light receding at unimaginable speed into a space that does not really exist, and nothing of what I have been tapping out here will be left. I would be looking at an empty, grey, death-coloured piece of plastic. No more of my wisdom, eloquence, anguish, sarcasm. And no possibility of subsequent, old-fashioned scrabblings in waste-paper baskets to bring any of it back. No searchings of bottom drawers for abandoned carbon copies. No dramatic midnight forays, while the rain comes down, into the rubbish bins outside. Not even a glimpse of one of those infinitely fragile sheets of crinkled, tinkling blackness (on which, before it breaks up into a thousand fragments, ghostly words may still be seen imprinted) that a fire might have left behind. Nothing.

But Foxborough? The fire that consumes him (cremation private, said the notice in *The Times*) will leave ash and smuts behind; and his latest wife; and his three sons by his three marriages; as well, of course, as his immortal works.

*

HAVE YOU TRANSFERRED TO DISK? A kindly question, a considerate one, for the machine to ask of me, before it permits me to cut off the power which keeps it alive. But when our own vital force fails no such option is offered to us. Nor indeed is there any DISK to which we could transfer any part of ourselves. For us, when the time comes, it is just a case of EDIT ABANDONED; and everything we have been conscious of, each last fragment of all we have ever experienced, is utterly and irrevocably erased.

Except for writers.

They, if you please, are the self-chosen, megalomaniac exceptions to this rule. The poets and novelists among them, at any rate, have decided that it is not going to apply to them. To the question HAVE YOU TRANSFERRED TO DISK? they alone can hope to give an unhesitating yes. Believe me, I know all their tricks. They cannot bear the thought of their precious experience going to waste. Their lives are not to be allowed simply to sink into the ground, fly away in smoke, fall out of sight, like everyone else's. Especially when they have the means (they think) of making something of it that time will not erode. Has not eroded.

*

Which is why I have no compunction about naming Foxborough. Promiscuously publishing writer-bastard that he was, he chose to make available to others his thoughts, his emotions, his innermost experience. So his shade can hardly complain about unwanted publicity now!

My best friend's case is quite different. True: nothing I do can make a difference to a man who has been kaput for so long; one who died unknown, uncelebrated, unpublished; unmarried and childless; 'survived by', as *The Times* would say, nobody and nothing. Well, virtually nothing. That is: me. Plus the bits and pieces of writing he did, which he occasionally referred to but never showed to anyone; not even to me.

Having been his only confidant (apart from the egregious Dr Laurence Fainman, who was paid for his services), I feel I owe it to him to protect his privacy still.

So, if I go on with this, I shall not reveal his name. Instead I plan to call him . . . something or other. I have not decided yet.

Then I can also let some of his poems be seen, at last.

*

Should I try to describe Foxborough? Not as when I saw him last (three or four years ago, it must be) walking among the gnarled, cliff-like buildings of Earls Court Square, with the branches of trees trailing about at all angles, like the random growth you might find at the bottom of a canyon, and cars stuffed bumper to bumper along the pavements, and a sodium glow clinging to every air-borne particle of moisture, and a deeper, fiercer, ruddier glare above, in the cavernous spaces of the London night-sky; and Foxborough – old, half-blind, carrying a white stick, uncertain of his feet, looking as if he had been strapped by an unkind nurse into the tight, leather-buttoned raincoat he was wearing – someone who should not have been out in that weather and at that hour, and yet even then still faintly suggesting the soldierliness of bearing that had once been his – no, not that Foxborough; but the one my friend had met, had been so pleased to meet, decades before?

The irony is that Foxborough looked so old to him then!

When you are twenty-two you do not know what 'old' means, you do not know what it looks like, you certainly know nothing about how it feels. You assume that anyone over forty must somehow be aware of the fact that effectively he is done for – a loser. You might be awed by him (by his power, his position, by the thought of how much, at such an advanced age, he must have been through); yet you will almost certainly see him as someone who has already spent most of the magic fund of possibilities and opportunities with which he had once been endowed. Now it is your turn. All these have now been passed on to you. They are like a weight within you that is also, mysteriously, a source of buoyancy. How pauperised anyone must feel who has lost them all, who has had them taken from him!

*

Diana, according to my friend, was quite different: different because he had no interest in her, aside from the fact that she was Foxborough's wife. He looked at her, when he first met her, only to try to see what had made him choose her, and to wonder if she was adequate to the position she occupied. Foxborough was unique, irreplaceable, the only person in the world who could have written the poems to which his name was attached. But what if the poet had never met *her*? Well, then he would have met some Sally or Penny or Joan, who would more or less have done for him and been to him what she was.

That is what he believed. That he should have done so reveals how thoroughly he had been infected by the megalomania of writers. You see, the world could grind on for another million years; but without him or her, this one or that (Keats or Shakespeare or Emily Brontë or Rodney Foxborough), it would find no substitute for what he and she alone, as individuals, had added to it. Prime Ministers and Lord Chancellors and Chief Justices can come and go; so do booking clerks in the railways and waitresses in your nearest pizza house; the same applies even to the greatest of scientists; there will always be other candidates for their jobs. (If Newton had not invented calculus, Leibniz would have done it – or did it.) But writers, real writers, writers who matter? Each of them is in a class of his own, or her own. They are indispensable to the work they do; hence, once they have made their appearance, they become irreplaceable to a world which had not even known beforehand how much it was missing their contributions to it.

*

To return, though, to the point where all this, everything, began: my friend's first sight of Foxborough.

The time: evening. The place: the hall of Nicodemus College, Cambridge (known generally as Nick's). The season: autumn. Moustached, tweed-jacketed, corduroy-trousered; aged twenty-two; of middle height; no slabs of flesh on his cheek-bones, no red veins in the whites of his eyes, no dry, fatigued wrinklings of the flesh on the back of his hands – there, at a long table, sits my lover-to-be; wholly unconscious of the fact that many decades later I will be trying to summon up a picture of him at just that moment. On either side of him, and across the long table, are other students. A man whom I shall call Cronin is there with his small, fine-featured, fine-skinned face, both brown and rose in hue, and his faintly trembling hands. (We shall be seeing more of him.) So is porcine Duggan, who breathes through an open mouth; and Dunnell, the long-legged pipe-brandisher; and suchlike. As for the rest – let them remain part of that anonymous mass which, for each of us, makes up a huge, populous hinterland of our consciousness, a kind of China of the mind.

Well, there they are, then, whoever they were or may have been; and there my friend is. Above him, black hammer beams hold up an almost gaudy ceiling of blue and gold and converging stripes of red. Against the panelled wall hang small portraits of unknown worthies – benefactors anyway – from the various centuries the college has been in existence. Recessed, arched windows of leaded glass show up black against the early evening sky. The high table is empty; the undergraduates are waiting for the Fellows to file in and the dinner to begin. The smell of food within the hall, where so many meals have been served for so many years, is heavy, meaty, warm, like the breath of an old dog who eats too much and takes too little exercise. To this friend of mine, sitting where he usually does, evening has brought not an appetite for food but an unfocused, familiar yearning – for what he does not know. Every evening brings it; brings the tightness in the chest that goes with it; the discontent in the mind; the hope lodged nowhere and everywhere within him.

There is a great scraping of feet and benches. The Fellows of the college have begun to enter, with the grey-suited, marching Master solemnly leading the procession. He carries his ponderous, grapefruit-coloured head before him, like a symbol of state. As they make their march up the hall, someone says to my friend, pointing, 'You see that man behind old Thompson. Over there. That's Foxborough, the poet.'

*

About that yearning I referred to a moment ago: that vague but intense evening appetite for another life, another self, another world to live in, which afflicted my friend. Leaving his homeland and coming to live in England had not, he had recently discovered, put it to rest. Perhaps nothing would. Sometimes it did indeed seem to find a focus; it would suddenly take adventitious form and shape. But each time it did so, some perverse trick of the mind ensured that that scene or moment, whatever it might be, seemed actually, dumbly longing for *him* to redeem it, and not the other way around.

It could be nothing more than a single line of bricks in an ancient wall, enclosing a hidden garden, with crumbling mortar between the bricks. How they would speak to him, if only they could!

Or a woman smiling as she stretches out a slender hand across a stall in a market, while the stallholder slowly drops her change into it, coin by coin. How incomplete they were without him!

Or it could be the leaf-laden limbs of a plane tree moving all at once in a gust of wind, each in a rhythm different from every other, none knowing, only he knowing, what a gracious, multiple whole they made.

*

Foxborough was in his bearded phase then (just as my friend was in his moustached phase). It was a peculiar beard: it sprouted

9

from every corner of his face and apparently in every direction at once; even upwards in places, it seemed, as well as down and outwards. As a result he looked as if he had thrust his face into a bag or bundle of hair. A luxuriant bundle it was: long, brown, lustrous, soft. The little that could be seen of his skin was pale; his eyes were dark and large. He was not a tall man, but his shoulders were broad and he walked upright, and sat upright, carrying his head back. His gaze was bold and yet somehow incurious.

So that was Foxborough! So that was what he looked like! That was what 'fame' made of you; and you of it! He stared and he stared: not because Foxborough was the first or most famous person he had seen, but because of the secret intimacy or complicity he felt with the man, or with his writings, and hence with the kind of fame he had. Somehow it seemed wholly right to my friend that he would not even have recognised the poet if his neighbour had not pointed him out. No one had told him that Foxborough was visiting the college; he had never seen a photograph of him with a beard.

*

The identity of that helpful neighbour at the table subsequently vanished from my friend's memory. He remains nobody in the story, an anonymous stranger, a creature of a single sentence. He was like an unseen soldier in an opposing army who fires a shot at random and, without ever knowing it, leaves an adversary forever scarred, recurringly in pain.

*

Foxborough and my friend did not meet that evening; the poet had not come to the college to speak at any of the student clubs, but on a private visit, so there was no occasion for an encounter between them. Nevertheless, they had eaten a meal in the same room; my friend had had a glimpse of him at his most affable and self-assured – drinking, smiling, wiping his mouth with a napkin, turning his square shoulders to the left and the right, as he engaged the people on both sides of him in conversation. Looking at Foxborough the sociable, the institutional, the success, among his contemporaries, a man whose appearance was remarkable only to the extent that he

10

himself had made it so by letting that absurd beard grow all over his face, indeed virtually conceal his face, my friend felt about him something more intense than the ordinary envy and patronage of the young. To him, Foxborough was the source and the carrier of a mystery. He had done it. This was the man who had written the lines that went through the heads of people he did not know, even as he sat there, indistinguishable from any other middle-aged visitor to the place. What secret power he had, in having no secrets!

*

It isn't her eyes or her hands I recall
but the smell at the roots of her hair,
and the swerve of each strand as it starts from her skull
*   and the white skin there.*

TWO

To the end of his life my friend remained convinced that if Foxborough had not been pointed out to him that evening, he would never have met him, or Diana. He had no faith in the magic of coincidence, synchronicity, and other such Jungian trash. It was (in his view) simply a statement of fact. A few weeks later he saw a small announcement in a newspaper about the last of a series of public lectures in the early evenings which Foxborough had been giving. This was during the Christmas vacation, part of which my friend was spending in the home of his college acquaintance Cronin, in North London. The venue – at some institution in the City, around the corner from the Bank of England – surprised him, and the glimpse he had had of Foxborough at the college had left him feeling both more curious and more proprietorial than before about the man. After all, he was one of his readers (of whom there could not be all *that* many); he had read him long before he had come to England; he had actually written an essay about his poems. Seeing Foxborough had been for him rather like seeing some other ancient and famous piece of England: a verification of the printed word or a solidification of the painted or photographed scene. It left you both disappointed and yet anxious for more.

So, on the spur of the moment, he made up his mind to go to Foxborough's lecture.

*

The institution at which Foxborough was to speak had an ancient name; but it turned out to have no premises at all. The lecture was given in a hall which belonged to one of the London livery companies. Outside, the winter-black streets roared, hissed, and glared, the outgoing tide of traffic swinging

12

now this way, now that. But the only sounds in the hall, which was big enough to seat several hundred people in stiff rows, were those of cautious coughings and bag-arrangings. By the time the lecture began, its audience consisted of a scattering of about twenty old and middle-aged people, a secretarial lady or two, a serge-suited porter who soon fell asleep, and a few schoolboys. From the walls hung wooden shields on which meaningless names were solemnly painted in gilt lettering; alongside the lofty windows were looped cords which must once have served to haul them open and closed. They had not been used, apparently, for many years.

Unaccompanied by any chairman or intercessor, Foxborough mounted the platform. He gazed despairingly around him, from behind an elaborate wooden lectern – all claws, balls, flutings, and a flat, tilted, submissive back. On this he placed the pages of his lecture, turned over one or two of them reflectively, and launched himself into it. He spoke rapidly, hardly looking up from his papers. His voice was dry; his accent refined; his 'r's defective but somehow proud. The man and his voice seemed to be at a distance from one another, let alone from the audience marooned in space before him. Throughout he gripped the lectern on both sides, letting go of it only to turn over a page.

All my friend was to remember of what he actually said, long afterwards, was a facetious two-line summary of a moment of crisis in a play by one of Shakespeare's contemporaries.

Villain: 'If you don't go to bed with me, I'll kill you right away.'

Heroine: 'Well, you can kill me as much as you like, but I'll never do it – so there!'

*

Afterwards he and Foxborough met in a pub nearby. He did not exactly follow the lecturer out of the hall – in fact, he reached the street outside before Foxborough emerged, and was standing there, hesitating which way to go, and what to do with himself, when the other passed him. Well-swathed in overcoat, scarf, flat hat, and beard, a brief-case in his hand, he too looked about him for a moment and then walked briskly down the middle of the

13

street, which was now in a trance-like calm after its rush-hour frenzy. He turned into a pub on the corner.

The temptation was too great for my friend to resist. By the time he entered the pub Foxborough was already sitting at a small, marble-topped table on which rested a tot of whisky, a pint of beer, and a newspaper carefully folded into a square wad. A pencil was in his hand. He was doing the crossword. His air was that of a man who had sat in this attitude, and engaged in this pastime, in just such surroundings, many times before. The pub, with its lustrous brown wood and sharp points of light from a multitude of bottles and mirrors, was quiet, almost empty, also enjoying its respite after the rush-hour.

My friend ordered a lager and stood at the counter, sipping at it. To his eye Foxborough looked more stern and imposing now, at his ease, on his own, preoccupied with his crossword puzzle, than he had in either of the two august halls in which he had seen him previously. Should he approach him? Would he look like a fool and supplicant if he did so? But if he did not make his move, how feeble he would later accuse himself of being! Another sip, another moment of hesitation, and he took two paces across the room.

'Mr Foxborough?'

'Yes?' – looking up.

'I – ahm – I've just been to your lecture.'

Foxborough stared at him. Close up, his eyes were lighter in colour than they looked from a distance: they were an indeterminate brown, with strange, mosaic-like chips of black set into them, as if at random. Perhaps that was the reason why there was something unresponsive or inexpressive about his gaze, almost like a blind man's. The skin around his eyes was pale, unlined, waxen in appearance. Yet it did not look unhealthy: it was too pure for that. Beneath it there sprang forward shamelessly that improbable, luxuriant, Muscovite beard.

'Well,' he said with a sudden, sardonic geniality, 'I'm pleased to meet you. I didn't know that anybody went to those lectures. I've given four altogether, and they get ghostlier and ghostlier each time. At first I thought the ghosts were all out there, in the audience; tonight, for the first time, I became convinced that *I* was the one who'd already . . . passed away.'

'Oh no,' my friend said, smiling. 'I didn't feel like a ghost. And you don't look like one to me.'

Foxborough considered this for a moment. Then, 'Sit down,' he responded, with a nod that flattened his beard momentarily against his chest.

My friend brought up a stool. Foxborough at once pushed his folded newspaper across to him. 'Can you see what sixteen down might be?'

'I'm useless at crosswords.'

'Try anyway.'

So he tried, unsuccessfully. *Salute a quick extra* in seven letters. Feeling that he had missed an important and unexpected chance to shine, he had to admit, no, it had him beat.

*

Did Foxborough do a great deal of lecturing? Had he ever had a full-time academic job? What did he think of writers or would-be writers taking up such jobs?

That was how it went: ploddingly. Foxborough was not forthcoming about himself, nor was he curious about the younger man. The only comment he made, on being told how he had been stared at during dinner in the hall at Nick's a few weeks before, was about the lukewarmness of the food that had been served to him there. What he most wanted, it seemed, was to go back to his crossword puzzle. So, after studying forlornly the few drops of brownish liquid still left in his glass, and the patterns of foam etched against the inner sides of it, my friend made up his mind to go.

He stood up. He told a lie. 'It's been very nice to meet you.' He told another lie. 'I really enjoyed the lecture.'

Foxborough lifted his strained, half-sightless eyes past him, indifferent to what he had just said.

'Diana!'

She came with a smell of the damp outside and cigarette smoke, with a handbag and a set of car keys thrown down casually on the bench nearby, with a clatter and gleam of bangles. Then there was her hair: copious, untidy, an improbable stiff

15

gold in colour, reaching almost to her shoulders. Then her lipsticked mouth, also copious. Then her large eyes.

'Goodbye!' Foxborough exclaimed at my friend suddenly. The shout of dismissal was so pointed and abrupt that the other simply stood there, not knowing where to look or how to make his departure. 'Goodbye!' Foxborough cried again, with a boyish scorn and impulsiveness. 'Don't you see? That's the answer to the clue. *Salute a quick extra* – they mean an extra in cricket. You know, a bye. A quick extra, a well-run extra, is a good bye! And goodbye is a salutation.'

'Oh.'

Then, in ordinary, collected fashion, Foxborough said, 'Goodbye,' and it was obvious from the way he turned to his wife that the word in his mouth no longer referred to his crossword puzzle.

THREE

Now for something more . . . profound. More historical. More diagnostic, shall we say? Even more prophetic, maybe. Some deep-o, cheap-o insights, anyway, into society and civilisation, for publishers and the rabble of reviewers to get their teeth into; not to speak of those dim but ambitious academics, Americans and otherwise. How else can one be recognised as a real writer: how else appear in television discussions on important issues, and look out with a cunning, tilted smile from the back pages of the Sunday papers? Damn it, as I sit here in front of this screen, processing these words, am I an 'unacknowledged legislator' of mankind; or am I not? Am I the spokeswoman for the moral conscience of *our culture*; or am I not?

So where to begin? The hunger for belief? (Always a winner.) Post-industrial society? The condition of women? The forthcoming extinction of the human race? *Anomie*?

*

The hell with it. Putting down what I know (and do not know) about Foxborough and Diana and that lover of hers, that lover of mine, is hard enough. The rest will have to wait.

They are all opaque to me: that is the truth. I do not understand what drove them to behave as they did, what they thought they were doing, what they really wanted. It baffles me still. This is true even of my friend, my confidant, my informant, without whom none of this could have been written.

Or perhaps, precisely because I have had the dubious privilege of receiving his confidences, he remains the most opaque of the lot.

Real writers, your genuine unacknowledged legislators and

wiseacres at large, are not supposed to say such things, I know, about 'their' characters. Everyone appearing in their pages is translucent to their piercing, writerly gaze. So are the rest of us. They shake their heads over the mistakes we make. They pour all over us the ineffable syrup of their compassionate understanding. They smile at our antics and self-deceptions. They palpate our deepest spiritual selves and then draw back to utter the solemn socio-historico-politico prognoses we are always so eager to hear, and which we are forever hoping will show us what we should feel, how to live, who we ultimately are.

Then it's hurrah for a multitude of readers, soulmates all (us again! always us!), out there in the lending-libraries, or among those half-tempted, half-begrudging scanners of the piles of new paperbacks in the bookshops.

Bliss!

Dear friends . . . Dear readers . . .

*

Jesus Christ, if I understood those people, would I still feel myself burdened with the miserable mystery of their lives?

*

Some facts about them, first of all.

To begin with Foxborough: not because he is more important than anyone else, but simply because he is the easiest one to deal with. All I need do is look up an old copy of *Who's Who* and there it all is, laid out for me.

FOXBOROUGH, Rodney James, poet and administrator, b. 1905, 2nd s. Mr Justice Desmond Foxborough and Emilia Foxborough (*Woodley*); m. (i) Sally Bredin (*Lanyon*) 1 s.; (ii) Diana Caroline (*Carter*) 1 s.; (iii) Annamaria Serena (*Sarkis*) 1 s. Educ: Westminster School and Christ Church, Oxford. Scriptwriter, PTA Motion Pictures, 1930-32; editor Stead & Egerton, publishers, 1932–6; lecturer, Helsinki University, 1936–9; War Service, Royal Artillery 1940–41, Intelligence Corps (Bletchley Park) 41–45; BBC producer (features) 46–50; BBC administrator (Staffing) 50–59; Staff Controller BBC World Service 1959 to retirement. Visiting Professor, Rutgers University, New Jersey, 1964; Visiting Fellow, Center for Behavioral Studies, Palo Alto, California, 1968. Publications:

An Impugned Axe (1929), poems; *Small Wars* (1933), poems; *The Grape Ladder* (1936), poems; *More Poems* (1946); *Bruised to Pleasure* (1953), poems; *Selected Poems* (1959); *Collected Poems* (1966); *Slakings* (1969); *First Essays* (1939); *Last Essays* (1971). Club: Athenaeum. Hobbies: walking, reading, disputing, murdering.

The last word of that entry is mine, by the way. Putting it there is a joke – of a kind. Anyway, it does not actually appear in any edition of *Who's Who*, so far as I know.

*

Next: Diana Caroline (Carter). No entry in *Who's Who* for her. So here is one, cobbled together for the occasion.

b. 1916, Srinigar, India, daughter of director of Far East merchanting house (Woodburne & Klisser) and tennis-playing, trophy-winning wife, also of family with Indian connections (civil service). Sent to boarding school in England at an early age. Left school in Dorset with no qualifications or certificates. Met her future husband just after the outbreak of war. 1 s. (conceived out of wedlock). Worked as typist in London office of father's company and then posted (as civilian) to Admiralty. Subsequently engaged in a variety of business enterprises, most of them with friends, all of a fairly small scale, some of them profitable, some not. Partner in a travel firm, ran a secretarial agency, invested money in and helped to edit a trade magazine (home decorating). Succeeded in ruining life of lover. Or so he claimed. Died in suspicious circumstances.

*

Lastly, the third point on this particular triangle: my friend. (b. 1934.) The man who, to his shame, to his chagrin, to his disbelief, fell irrevocably in love, not long after his twenty-second birthday, with a woman almost twenty years older than himself.

For him let me offer an epitaph rather than an entry in the *Who's Who* that never was.

Oh him? Adrian Bester? He's the guy who fell in love with a woman twenty years older than he was. She was married to some poet, I think. She actually had a kid who was about his age.

*

That is the story, in essence. There is not much to add to it, aside from a few details, like a murder – and grief – and silence

19

– and money wasted on psycho-analytical sessions – and a career of fits and starts – and compulsive confession – and now this, here, in front of me, these green ghosts of letters and words appearing out of a non-space.

None of it should have happened! Everything should have gone differently! That is what he continued to believe, long after 'everything' had taken place. It was all a kind of mistake, an error of understanding, which he would somehow be able to put right: if not now, then retrospectively; if not in the past, then prospectively, next time.

No use to tell him that there is no next time, that nothing can be put right once it has happened, because the past itself is nowhere and nothing, and has no more reality than the ghostly, spaceless arena in which these words seem to appear. He knew that. Who does not?

But knowing it made no difference to what he felt, or failed to feel, or to his unshakeable conviction about another kind of nowhere-space: the world of what should have been.

*

I see that I have given his name away. It had to be done at that point, I suppose. Impossible to write an epitaph for someone without granting him or her the dignity of a name.

Still, I shall mostly go on as I have so far, referring to him simply as 'my friend'. That is how I almost always spoke of him to people who did not know him. 'I'm going on holiday with my friend.' 'They had me and my friend to stay for a few days.' 'My friend was meant to be reading the map, but we got hopelessly lost, all the same.'

Like that. A long time ago.

*

You know what this Adrian Bester, this friend of mine, was – by origin?

He was an Afrikaner. A Boer. A member of that race who have for so long been famous chiefly for oppressing other people at the foot of the African continent.

Not a nice thing to have to confess about so close a friend, is it? Especially when I add that he was not and never would have been one of your renegade, radical, self-sacrificing, freedom-fighting

20

Boers, your premature warriors against apartheid and injustice, your early dreamers of multi-racial dreams.

No, he was . . . how shall I put it? Fatigued? Irritated? Selfish? Escapist? Claustrophobic?

That kind of Afrikaner. There are some: many more now than there were when he was a young man. But you find such men and women in every besieged group, every people whom history has by the throat, every struggling, provincial culture. Basically, they feel put upon. They want to be left alone. They do not want to be answerable to anybody or for anybody but themselves. The national or racial obligation to feel like this, to be lumped with that, to defend this, to attack that – or, for that matter, to do the exact opposite of any of these – is one they would like to repudiate: for ever. Ditto the expectations that people of other races and nations have of them.

As a result they are prone to irony, self-hatred, and an inveterate disloyalty, or at least scepticism, not only towards that which they dislike, but also, and even more remarkably, towards whatever they are attracted to.

It is quite natural that other members of their own group and of alien groups should be inclined to excoriate them. But it is also a waste of effort: such people, the disaffected ones, do the job of self-excoriation much better than anyone else ever could. It is also a waste of time sentimentalising them: they do that job, too, better than anyone else. In certain high, romantic moods they like to see themselves as permanent outsiders who know the sad truth about man and society better than any insider ever could. At other times they are simply full of resentment and envy.

Altogether, they are probably much more trouble than they are worth. I mean, to themselves as well as to everyone else.

*

So see my friend at the age of seventeen, sitting on the verandah of a smallish, tin-roofed house, bungalow-style, in a residential street of a town called Bloemfontein. He has a book in his hand. It is a sunny afternoon in May: late autumn it happens to be, in that ill-placed part of the world. Little traffic passes along the street, though it is not far from the centre of town. Parched-looking jacaranda trees, planted at intervals along the

21

pavement, lift their twigs to an inflexibly blue sky. The wall behind the young man is plastered white; the roof above the verandah is held up by square brick pillars; the garden consists of a square of grass, already turning brown at the approach of winter, and several fruit trees of modest size. From one of them pomegranates hang; the tough rind of each fruit is split open to reveal pink but blackening teeth inside, fixed in a meaningless grin. African voices, from the back of the house, or the house next door, are engaged in an interminable conversation, at once vigorous and mild, in a language he cannot even name, let alone understand. The couch he sits on has been demoted from indoors, so no one cares now if its covers become even more faded in the sun than they already are; or if, rolling over to lie on his stomach, his book still firmly in his hand, he digs his shoes even more deeply into its sagging springs and stuffing.

The book is Joyce's *A Portrait of the Artist as a Young Man*; and Stephen Dedalus's adolescence, described in swooningly parodistic-romantic prose, has proved to be so unrewarding, such heavy going, that he has been tempted more than once to abandon the task of reading it. But his own adolescence, as well as Stephen's, is at stake here. His pride, his half-formed but obdurate idea of himself as an intellectual and a reader of hard books, his determination to be able to say to others that he has read the damn thing, together with his hope of at last finding out why so many literary *eminenti* have declared it to be so important, a great work of art, a classic – all this helps to keep him going. In any case, the swooning passages now appear to be over; instead the book has grown more like an argument and less like a novel, and after the tedium of the previous section this is an improvement.

And there on the page, quite unexpectedly, Stephen Dedalus speaks not only to another character in the novel, but directly to him, to this young man in Bloemfontein. 'I shall express myself as I am,' Stephen says. 'When the soul of a man is born in this country there are nets flung at it to hold it back from flight. You talk to me of nationality, language, religion. I shall try to fly by those nets.'

That is all. It is enough. Much moved, slightly afraid, full of envy for someone who could think such things for himself, instead of finding them already printed for him in the pages of a book by someone else, my friend puts the novel face downwards on the red-dyed, polished cement of the verandah-floor. He does not look at his surroundings; rather, they suddenly and silently reassert themselves. Trees in the garden. A low brick fence. A dove cooing insistently. Sunlight colder than before and yet more syrupy in colour; somehow more syrupy in texture too. Now a rattletrap van storms down the street. The iron roofs of the houses on the other side are a dull red in colour.

You talk to me of nationality, language, religion. I shall try to fly by those nets.

Me too. I must. I will.

*

A sensitive Boer, you think? I agree. A disaffected one? Certainly. But an ambitious one, too, I would say.

There will never be an end, it seems, to these ambitious young people from the provinces; and to the disappointments they are bound to inflict on themselves. His attempt to 'fly by those nets' takes him to an (English-language) university in South Africa. It makes him do well in his chosen course. It brings him to Cambridge, to London, to the heartland of his people's ancient enemy. He has won a scholarship which he was free to take up anywhere in Europe. He could have gone to Holland or Germany or to wicked France. But at no time, at least at no time before his meeting with Diana, did he regret his choice of England. Indeed, he has made up his mind to stay on in England, once he has taken his second degree. It has become his aim to lose himself, to change himself, to vanish into the crowd; and nowhere can this be more readily done, it seems to him, than in England. Especially since the freakishness of history has given him the automatic right of British citizenship and of residence in Britain, if he chooses to exercise it. (For so the law ran, in those days.)

Yet it remains his aim also to stand out, somehow, from the crowd; to have a distinguished and enviable career. Such contradictions are commonplace, as most of us know only too well. He has not yet really made up his mind how he

23

is going to do it; but he has at least decided how it is *not* going to be done. He is not going to try to find any kind of literary employment, his enthusiasm for certain kinds of poetry and fiction notwithstanding. Oh, he writes, of course: stories, bits of plays, poems; poems especially. But nothing he has ever written, neither in English nor in Afrikaans, neither in prose nor verse, has seemed to him worthwhile. And if that is the case, and if (as he fears) it is doomed to remain the case, then the idea of making a living as a literary hanger-on, a reviewer or critic or scholar or publisher, has no appeal at all. It would be as intolerable to him as being the 'best friend' of a woman he loves.

That was his own analogy, I should say: thought up by the man himself, at the time. Not by me, now.

Better by far, it seems to him, to keep his distance. So the law is what he is studying. A barrister is what he hopes to become. And these decisions taken, he finds them positively to his advantage in meeting the would-be poets, novelists, dramatists and suchlike among his Cambridge contemporaries. He knows as much as they do about their passions and predilections; and at the same time he is learning about tort and equity.

*

But it is just as well for his peace of mind that none of his contemporaries know that twice a week, late in the afternoons, he pays a visit to a house of blackish and yellow Cambridge brick, with diminutive manorial protuberances, on the far side of Parker's Piece. There, in the presence of a lady of quite advanced years, he performs certain exercises of a shameful kind.

No, it is not sexual 'relief' he gets from her. (That he mostly still gets from himself, *faute de mieux*.) What she offers him is something far more shameful. He goes there for elocution lessons. The lady is trying to train him out of producing, every time he opens his mouth, those thudding, crashing Afrikaans consonants native to him, the swallowed Afrikaans vowels which he and others might have taken for granted in Bloemfontein, but which he has come to be ashamed of here.

As I said, he is ambitious. He is busy trying to 'fly by those nets'. Hard work this net-flying-by process always has been,

24

and will be, and especially so when the nets you wish to avoid have somehow been incorporated in the very move-ments of your throat and tongue, the unconscious contrac-tions, elongations, and resonatings of your throat and vocal chords.

His flying-by coach, Miss Gwynneth Timpkins, is small, slightly built, round-chinned, fine-nosed; she wears rimless spec-tacles, white blouses, and skirts down to her ankles; her voice is soft and so is her skin; even the wrinkles on it look soft. Altogether, to his eye she is like an escapee from an Edwardian novel; but then, it sometimes seems to that infatuated eye of his that half the people in England are on parole from the pages of some book or other. (Often enough from a book he has never even read.) He knows that Gwen, as she has encouraged him to call her, used to work in provincial repertory, before settling in Cambridge as a teacher of speech and drama; he knows also that Regan in *King Lear* was once her favourite role. She does not look much like Regan to him; but he has to believe it when he sees her acting out bits of the play for his benefit, with much striding back and forth across the limited space of her 'studio', and spasmodic clutchings at the sides of her long skirt.

Gwen, it turns out, has several unusual pedagogic theories, some of which she puts into practice with him. Among them is her belief that the reading of Chaucer's verse aloud, in the accent sup-posedly used in the poet's day, will serve to loosen his tongue and re-train the muscles of his throat as nothing else can. So behold our Bloemfontein boy, his dubious moustache on his upper lip and his hungry heart somewhere in his boots, standing in the middle of the room, between the piano and the gas fire, looked down on by Gwen's framed theatrical photographs and program-mes, reciting to the beat of that lady's delicate, upraised finger:

> 'Ne deeth, allas! ne wol nat han my lyf;
> Thus walke I, lyk a restless catyf,
> And on the ground, which is my modres gate,
> I knokke with my staf, bothe erly and late,
> And seye, "leve moder, leet me in!"'

25

He had never 'done' Chaucer at school or university, and he was never to read him again in later years. Of all the passages he recited to Gwen only that one remained in his memory: the cry of a man looking for death, knocking on the earth, his 'mother's gate', and appealing to her to let him in. Many years later this was to be one of his party pieces: at special request he would recite the lines in the accent taught to him by Miss Timpkins, together with exaggerated versions of the gestures she had encouraged him to make.

Then death obliged him. His mother-earth answered his knock. She opened her gate to him.

No more recitations.

*

As for his real mother, back in Bloemfontein – of her I know very little. I have seen a few photographs of her, alone or alongside other members of the family. Looking at them I recognise more of him in her than in any of the others. Neat but converging brows they shared, and sturdy shoulders, and an anxious, ingenuous expression. She, whose body had once constituted the very net in which he had hung, the gate through which he had once been expelled into the world, was to see little enough of him after he left for England. She saw him just once, I believe, when he went home for a few months after graduating. The next time he returned it was to attend her funeral. She died relatively young – of cancer in the breast; the breast at which, in another unimaginable life, in another unimaginable form, he had once suckled.

Suckled too much? Suckled too little? Too hard? Too timidly? Tell me, Dr Freud, was it there, in Bloemfontein, at that Afrikaner lady-teacher's breast (where another boy and two girls had preceded him) – was it there determined that he should fall in love, two decades later, and in another country, with a woman just old enough to be his mother? Was it then that his fate was settled? And if he had not met Diana, would some other mother, some other ex-giver of suck, have inevitably captured him?

Or is it Dr Melanie Klein, supposedly the real expert in such sucking, fucking matters, that I should be consulting?

*

26

Let me jump ahead briefly, then, to further private meetings between my friend and another kind of teacher; another spiritual consultant and adviser, anyhow. This one, Dr Laurence Fainman by name, 'orthodox' by self-description, lived in a red-brick house in Hampstead, with white-sashed windows looking over a handsome garden and a tree-lined street. It was through the garden, and by a side-entrance, that Dr Fainman's patients were encouraged to approach his consulting room.

The doctor was the owner not only of that house in Hampstead, but also of several suits of an inexpressive, dark blue shade; a large, bald forehead, also inexpressive; features to match; and long fingers which he had a habit of pressing together at the tips. Then he rested his chin on them.

The scrupulous nakedness of that chin showed that the orthodoxy to which Dr Fainman subscribed would not have been recognised as such by his pious Hasidic ancestors. To him my friend told some things which I daresay he never told to anyone else, not even to me; or perhaps not at such length and not in quite the same way. What he dreams about, for example. Who he would like to kill, and how. What fantasies come into his mind when he masturbates. Which of his sisters he liked best, and why. The cut of his father's trousers and his infantile speculations about what they concealed. And suchlike. And, over and over again, Diana, Diana, Diana, not-yet-dead Diana.

*

Staring into this flat, black screen that stares at me, while I endlessly tattoo these lines of ghostly green letters across it; knowing more, simply by virtue of the passage of time, than either he or Dr Fainman did, I marvel at what it is to have the advantages of hindsight.

How sagacious it makes one feel! And how helpless.

FOUR

Another long gone, long dead domestic scene, then, of which I find myself compelled to make my present business.

There he is again, my friend or enemy, not as I remember him, but as he told me he had been, before I had any consciousness of him as an individual – there he is, standing on the doorstep of the Foxboroughs' house in Dulwich. It is a Sunday afternoon in late February. Two long months have passed since he attended that lecture given by Foxborough in the City. After an exchange of letters and a couple of telephone calls, he has come to see the poet. He has brought with him for autographing three of Foxborough's volumes of verse; also a tape recorder and a list of questions he proposes asking the poet, so that he might write up the visit for a student magazine, OMEGA, which is edited by that college-friend of his, Cronin.

A big deal, you see. At least it seems so for a poetry-loving, Foxborough-admiring young man from South Africa: one who has no intention, I repeat, of setting himself up as a writer, but who nevertheless arrives at that particular doorstep full of curiosity, ambition, and social hunger. The occasion has been carefully figured out by him. He has drafted the questions he is going to put to the poet in the course of the interview; he has also drafted (in his own mind) some of the answers which he hopes the poet will make to those questions. He has rehearsed the modest smile and the dismissive movement of the arm with which he will brush away the compliments the poet will pay him at the penetrating nature of his queries. In his mind (yet again) he has nodded wisely at certain unexpected confessions of weakness and unhappiness which the poet will make to him, and he has promised to include nothing of them

28

in the published version of the interview. Indeed, so eager is he to be the recipient of those confessions, he has already promised never to say anything about them to anyone.

But in none of his hopes and fantasies is there an inkling of what is actually about to take place.

*

Damp because of the drizzle falling from without, as well as the sweat rising from within, a strand of his dun-coloured hair sticking to his faintly freckled brow, he composes himself on the Foxborough doorstep. He passes the brief-case he is carrying from one hand to the other and takes a deep breath. As he presses the doorbell, he allows an eagerly rehearsed phrase of greeting to rise from his breast to his open lips.

Where it dies unuttered. Foxborough is not there.

Diana, who has come to the door, explains that a colleague has unexpectedly called him away. On a BBC matter. He has left his apologies and a promise to fix up another date some time in the future.

My friend stands on the doorstep. He has nothing to say for himself. He feels a fool, of course, and something worse than that. In his heart, among all his charred expectations, lies the black, hot conviction that he has just been snubbed. Mercilessly. And underneath that there is a half-formed conviction of yet another kind: that a snub is exactly what he deserves. He should not have tried so hard; he should not have permitted himself all those paltry fantasies.

Some of what he feels, enough of it, is plain to Diana. She does not really remember him, but her husband has told her about the visitor he had been expecting, and she knows who he is and vaguely recalls where she had last seen him. So she takes pity on him and asks him in. Having come all the way from North London, and through such murky weather, wouldn't he stay to have a cup of coffee? Or a drink?

'I've come from Cambridge, actually,' he confesses.

Whether this is intended to make her feel worse about his disappointment, or to make himself feel worse about it, he does not know.

Anyhow, he stays; and his life changes irrevocably. They sit in the living-room. They have a cup of coffee. Later he has a drink. Though it is quite dark outside, the curtains have not been drawn. The black panes of glass in the bay window contain a tilted, fragmented, wholly fictional version of the room they are sitting in. There, shining with a strange forlornness among bare branches and bits of left-over daylight, appear random reflections of armchairs in floral covers, improbably angled to snatches of bookshelves, rugs, framed canvases and prints. And also some disjointed portions of themselves: hands *sans* arms; heads *sans* eyes.

Late Saturday afternoon, in a comfortably unimposing, sub-urban setting: one wholly appropriate, it might be thought, to a senior administrator in the World Service of the BBC. That he is also a poet, and, in the tiny world of poetry writers and readers, a well-known one, would not have been evident to the visitor. But then, how should a poet indicate the nature of his vocation to outsiders? By leaving sheets of manuscript lying around? Or empty gin bottles? Or phials of morphine?

Or by showing no surprise at finding his wife on the floor, in the arms of a man twenty years younger than herself?

*

No, that is not what happened. Foxborough finding them on the floor, I mean. It is merely what my friend feared might happen, once he and she were lying on it.

But he got away safely. Unscathed.

At least, he thought then that that was how he had got away. His feelings about what had happened were chiefly amusement; astonishment; pride; gratitude; condescension. The one he felt most condescending of all toward was not Diana, however, or her husband, but himself, the ignorant young fellow he had been a few hours before: the man who had travelled up from Cambridge with his brief-case in his hand and a list of questions about poetry in his pocket, little dreaming of what was to follow.

And as for that Bloemfontein hobbledehoy of centuries before, latitudes distant, who had first come across Foxborough's name and some of his poems in an anthology given to him by a homosexual English master — ! Pathetic, he had been, that

30

youngster; quite pathetic. (The English master too, come to think of it.) Yet he must also have been an oddly promising boy. Look how he had transformed himself, and what he had just managed to achieve, after all.

*

They had sat there, he and Diana, talking as strangers do: politely, attentively, at first conscious of little but their ignorance of one another, of their fear of boring and of being bored; then conscious also, on both sides, of a growing sense of ease and self-assurance. It was not difficult for them to be alone together, for all the differences of age and background between them: that was the first discovery they made about each other. He talked about what he thought of Cambridge, and of his plans to be admitted to one of the Inns of Court, once he had graduated. She refrained from asking him about the political and racial situation in South Africa, for which he was duly grateful. She spoke about her son, who was a weekly boarder at Westminster School, as his father had once been. Later she told him that she was working a few days a week, until something better turned up, in a local hardware shop.

'A *hardware* shop?' he said, much surprised.

'Yes – you know – paints, screws, electrical appliances, that kind of thing.' Then, with a note of mockery which he at once knew he had invited: 'Don't look so dismayed. It's a very respectable occupation, I promise you.'

To explain or excuse himself he said, 'Yes, but it's not very – well, glamorous, is it? I mean . . .'

'Well?' she asked, as his voice trailed away, 'what do you mean?'

He had wanted to say, 'I mean, it's not very glamorous for the wife of a famous poet.' But he feared she might take offence at being seen as nothing more than an adjunct to her husband. He began yet again: 'I mean, for someone – ' Nothing came to his mind that did not sound wrong and snobbish: even worse than the phrase he had just rejected.

Whereupon, out of his silence, out of this trivial embarrassment, there sprang some demon instinct to flatter, to lie, to cut a figure. It took his tongue. It made him say, 'For someone who *is* so glamorous.'

He looked up and found himself staring into her eyes; and, by God, what he saw there was that his lie had suddenly become the truth. She looked beautiful to him. Her eyes were full of light and amusement – and, it seemed to him, experience too; steeped in a knowing and yet youthful blueness he had not seen there before. Yet the blue in them was grey also.

Into the renewed silence he said, as if trying to backtrack, but too late, 'I don't think I've ever met anyone who works in a hardware shop. That is . . . I've never met one outside a hardware shop.'

Her laugh was deep and abrupt, almost cough-like; her right hand flew into her hair, and pushed it back above her forehead. It was stiff, thick, rather coarse-fibred, that hair of hers; it would never stay in place; the natural spring of it had been crushed by too many years of ruthless perming and dyeing.

'You have led a sheltered life,' she said.

Once again he was provoked to a revelation he did not understand and could not resist. 'My father died when I was nine. I saw him do it. He had a heart attack in front of me.'

It was something he had never spoken of to anyone before; not in all the years since it had happened. Her mouth opened in a movement of sympathy that produced no sound. Yet there remained a faint gleam of mirth, too, in her eyes.

*

Think of them not as etiolated by time, taken apart by death, marooned in the irrecoverability of the past, dependent upon another (i.e. me) for an existence as shadowy and transparent as that of their own reflections in the branches of the trees outside, pierced by bleak points of light from other houses. Think of them as they were to themselves – breathing, waiting, doubting, alert, conscious of a change having taken place in the relation between them, neither knowing what the change was or what it might mean; immersed in that which is forever the essence of the present moment: ignorance of what is to come.

See the skin wrinkling at her plump wrists, as she picks up her cup, drinks from it, and puts it down. Hear the fine little screech the base of the cup makes as it finds its place on the saucer. See her hands go to her lap, and then between her knees. She wears black trousers and a white sweater with a roll collar. Sometimes her chin disappears into it. Her skin is without lustre; all the more so, it seems, because of the bright, false sheen of her hair. On her brow are some faint lines, presaging the wrinkles to come. The bangles she had worn the last time he had seen her are gone; in their place is a single thin silver bracelet. Behind her, in the window, hangs a reflection of my friend's head. It is round and almost featureless, and seems to look on her from the back, with a blurred gaze. As if aware that she is being spied on from behind (but never guessing that another might spy on them both, decades later!), she gets up and draws the curtains. They are made of coarsely woven cloth, with strong bars of red and grey and black running across them, which meet where the curtains join. She returns to the couch on which she has been sitting, but does not at once take her place on it. Instead she leans over him, takes his face in her hands, and kisses him on the lips.

His heart beats fiercely. He feels a boyish warmth at the back of his neck; but no desire. He does not move. She looks at him gravely, from above, apparently considering what she has done. Again, and yet as if for the first time, he sees how large her eyes are, how veined are their whites, how much slate there is in their blueness.

'I'm not frightened of you,' he says, with only the faintest hint of a tremor in his voice.

'No,' she agrees; still pensive, and yet still somehow, in the depths of herself, amused. 'There's no reason why you should be.'

*

But there were such reasons, of course. Otherwise he would never have said it. There was nothing arcane about those reasons, either.

He hardly knew her. She was much older than he was. She had taken the initiative, in kissing him. She was a married woman. Her husband was a famous poet. She was the mother of an adolescent boy.

Also, she was English – in her own house; among her own

33

possessions; at home in every sense of the word; the enunciator without effort of consonants and vowel sounds he was taking lessons in a vain effort to emulate. He was the outsider, the uncouth but ambitious colonial – inside the room and yet in blurred, faceless fashion outside it, looking in, like a ghost.

However, as things turned out, what he should really have feared was the tiny glimpse he had of the moisture in her mouth, as she opened her lips to speak again. The light was darkness there. The darkness gleamed.

For a moment he could see nothing else. And then, for some reason he could not understand, he never was to understand, he had to fear even more the pang he felt at the simple, delayed, turn of her head, as she lowered her chin into the thick collar beneath it, and looked away; sadly it seemed. Then the movement was over. She had nothing to say.

*

It is not my plan to become a pornographer of the small screen: this particular little screen, that is; the one on which these words appear. Since I am driven to try to re-create what they went through, the voyeur's role is actually forbidden to me. To try to picture our partners or the partners of others in the flexures and complicities of passion, their eyes glazed or averted, their limbs open or clasping – all this, precisely in being recollective and anticipatory, is bound to be pornographic as well. But doing is different. Doing knows only the present; it is without past and future; it is fierce and busy; even at the moments of its greatest intensity it remains remorselessly matter-of-fact, peculiarly resistant to the very fantasies which have helped to bring it about and which will later be fed from it.

One thing led to another. He had her in his arms. They sank to the floor. Though their eyes embraced, they did not witness their embraces. They could not witness them. Later he remembered one particular moment: opening his eyes suddenly, and flinching from the brightness of the light, with Diana above him, her weight on him, he saw a white-painted shelf above a nearby radiator, on which there stood a collection of tiny glass bottles of different colours, and, of all things, a turquoise-coloured china hippopotamus.

34

This, while he gripped and pressed on the fierce, soft pressure that gripped and pressed on him, he to surround her, she to surround him.

How different everything was from what it should have been!

*

I was not there, I saw none of it, I lived unconscious of it; and that is why I now haunt it and am haunted by it – me, the rememberer of another's memories, faithful but unwilling guardian of times, places and incidents which exist today solely because I feel compelled to recall them.

So it is not for me, of all people, to rebuke him for the kind of curiosity he felt about her, subsequently – much though I would like to do so; or to blame him for believing that curiosity of his to be harmless and inevitable, of no real consequence. Anyone in his position would have felt it. The questions which came to his mind were obvious enough. Why him? Why then? What had gone before? He was not vain enough to believe that she had been struck by a *coup de foudre* at the sight of him. Was it, then, that she was unfaithful to Foxborough whenever she got the chance? And if so, for how long had it been going on? Did he know of it? Did he care? Did he do the same to her?

Inevitable questions, as I say; none of which, not even in mangled or euphemistic form, he had the nerve or the time or even the desire to put to her before leaving the house. Now, as he rode in an underground train back to Liverpool Street Station, they and others like them, along with a variety of vague speculations and precise but fleeting images, passed in random disorder through his mind. The train jolted forward to the accompaniment of elaborate shrieks and squeaks, as if an entire orchestra of percussion, brass and wind was at work in the tunnel. Solid black balls suspended on springs wagged in admonitory fashion from the ceiling of the coach he was sitting in. Nobody was holding on to them; there were just a few people in the carriage, all of whom, scattered at random across the seats, had carefully composed themselves around their own secrets. At his crotch, there was a faint dampness.

And her secrets? What was she doing now? And thinking?

What had she been doing all the years he hadn't known her?
And the years before he had been born?

Now there was a thought!

But of his own change of heart, of mind, of being, at that
moment when she had been about to speak and had instead
lowered her brazen head and suddenly sombre face, almost as
if to hide it from him – of that moment he chose not to think.
He felt that it was Diana's actions that needed to be explained;
not his own. It was as if he was no mystery to himself. Surely
he had behaved as men were expected to behave when such
opportunities presented themselves. The problem or puzzle was
all on her side.

Or so he believed. Or wished to believe.

FIVE

Some days later he had a note from Foxborough, apologising for his absence on the afternoon when they had arranged to meet, and inviting him to a party a fortnight hence. The letter was in Foxborough's hand, on BBC notepaper, with a line drawn through the letterhead and the address in Dulwich written beneath. Quite a formal note it was. *Please accept my apologies . . . I hope you will let me make amends . . . Perhaps you would care to join my wife and myself . . .'*

My wife and myself?

'I hope she doesn't begin to make a nuisance of herself,' he said aloud in his empty room.

He had just returned there after lunch in hall, having picked up the letter on the way. He read the note again, indeed several times over, looking for clues to special meanings that may have been hidden within it. Then he returned it to the envelope it had come in, went to his bookshelf, and carefully put it in one of the volumes of Foxborough's verse which he had taken to the house, in the hope that he might get the poet to sign it. Now he had garnered not merely a signature; but a letter, a veritable collector's item.

'You have no scruples,' he said aloud once again, addressing himself in a satisfied tone of voice.

The book he was holding had a chaste typographical cover; it had been bought second-hand in a bookshop in Cape Town; he had written his name and the date of the purchase on the flyleaf, under the name of the previous owner, a certain P.J. Stockdale. He had no idea who this P.J. Stockdale was and could not begin to imagine what he had made of the poems; but he was quite certain, and childishly gratified at being so

37

certain, that P.J. Stockdale had never, not once, made love to the poet's wife on the floor of the poet's living-room.

That did it. He responded on college notepaper. *Dear Mr Foxborough. Thank you for your invitation for 12th March. I shall be delighted to come.* Then his signature. Then a P.S. *Please give my kind regards to Mrs Foxborough.* Followed by a reconsideration of the matter, a crumpling up of the note, and a second version of it without the P.S.

*

On the appointed evening, wearing his only suit, he stood once more in the Foxborough doorway. It had a peaked, Gothicky, wooden hood above it: something which he had quite forgotten, but now remembered all the more sharply for that very reason. He had considered bringing with him a bottle of wine, but had rejected the idea: it was the kind of gesture one made towards one's friends, one's peers, not towards old, well-established, apparently prosperous people like the Foxboroughs. He had also thought of buying a bunch of flowers for Diana; but had decided against that too. Nothing was to be taken for granted by him; nothing was to be suggested or implied by him; not at any rate until he had seen how he was received by her.

There was the doorbell, just as before, set into the bricks of the wall. Under his feet was the same doormat. Out in the street the sodium lamps sent out the same crawling, all-coating, orange-purple light as when he had left, last time.

On this occasion, however, Foxborough answered his ring. But it was a wonderfully changed, plain, pallid, youthful, clean-shaven, businesslike Foxborough who stood there. His beard had been doffed as if it had been nothing more than an item bought from a joke-shop. The hair on his head seemed suddenly to have been revealed: it was dark, thick, orderly, with a strong wave to it. His long upper lip showed itself prominently.

The visitor stared forward in silent astonishment, and so did Foxborough, who plainly had no notion of who this man might be. From the rear, presumably from the very room in which he and Diana had made love to one another, came the smell and the noise of the party. They were inextricably mixed together. It was as if the gin produced that sound, the voices that piercing, sweetish odour.

*

'I'm – '

'Oh yes, of course, come in, come in. Bester, isn't it? From Cambridge?'

Foxborough stood aside. His guest passed him in the hallway.

'I don't know how many people you'll recognise,' Foxborough said. 'But you know Diana. She was very keen that you should come.'

'Oh,' he said, confused, 'that's nice.'

The room burst upon him: light, talk, people. Most of them, he noticed at once, looked quite old. Many of the men had bald heads, or grey hair growing over the shafts of their spectacles; many of the women had beefy shoulders and bosoms that sagged down of their own weight, hammock-fashion, despite being trussed from above and below. He knew nobody there – other than Diana, who, after what seemed to him a long time, noticed him and at once came over, through the throng. She met him with an unembarrassed smile and a steady gaze, like an old friend rather than an accomplice.

'I'm glad you came,' she said. 'Rodney was so sorry to have missed you, last time. He was determined you should come tonight.'

'Was he? And you?'

Her smile softened. 'I had no objection.'

A girl dressed in a white top and a black skirt brought up a tray laden with glasses of wine. It was impossible to judge from her appearance whether she was merely being helpful or was paid for what she was doing. Her head of fair hair had obviously been washed for the occasion. 'Red or white?' she asked. 'There's gin and whisky too, over at the table, if you want it.'

'Whisky, please.'

'I'll go and get it,' Diana said, but she had no sooner set out to do so than she was waylaid by one of her guests.

In this way, for him, the party began. Much of it was like

any other party he might have gone to where he knew few or no people: boring and tense, awkward and of no consequence. His perceptions were simultaneously sharpened and blurred by the drink he took. There were faces attractive, forbidding, fatigued; scraps of food eaten at awkward angles; words lost in the din; sudden moments of awareness of the usurped, domestic life of the room, waiting quietly to return from the corners left to it. He recognised a few people there from having seen their pictures in the papers or on the television. There was a poet far more famous than Foxborough, and a few other writers with reputations as well-established as their host's; an actress whom he had last seen in a Chekhov performance in the West End; a philosophy don whose opinions on such topics as capital punishment and abortion were constantly canvassed by the press. He spoke to none of these eminences, but managed to hold his own with some of the others there. A woman who worked in the social services had a long conversation with him about the social services; someone from the BBC did the same about the BBC; a neighbour of the Foxboroughs revealed that she had spent several years in Cape Town. And an American with thick golden hair and immaculate teeth, accompanied by an admiring female novelist half his size, announced to the group around him that he had 'shamanistic powers'. He had, he revealed, felt them come upon him in great strength that very afternoon, in St Albans Abbey. And he held up his arms, clothed in checked tweed, his fists clenched like cauliflowers at the end of them, to show how it had happened. Whereupon the novelist held his arm even more tightly than before.

She believed it. He believed it. My friend envied and despised them both.

Was the party thinning out? Should he be thinking of going? What was the point of his being there? He certainly had not come across the beautiful women, the brilliant and engaging men, whom any novice might hope to find, and make an impression on, at the first London party he goes to. Neither Foxborough nor Diana had spoken to him since his arrival, though both had repeatedly acknowledged his presence with a nod or a smile or the offer of another drink, another plate of food. He had not forgotten that each of them had placed the responsibility for inviting him on the other; but he had failed in his attempt to challenge Diana on this subject. There were too many other people in earshot; too many demands on her attention.

*

Definitely, it was time to go. These people had a life of their own: friends, position, a past, assumptions they took for granted. For reasons as banal to her, no doubt, as his own were to him, he and Diana had shared a moment of secret intimacy, and all that went with it (sighs, warmth, effort, clutchings, slime). So what? He did not even know how secret those moments still were. Seeing her full body in the rich, high-necked dress she was wearing, with its little Chinese collar, the silken material splashed and daubed with reds and yellows like a painter's palette, he wondered if she had told Foxborough about what had happened between them. It was possible. Anything was possible between such strangers. A stranger was all she was to him. She was taller than he had expected her to be, perhaps because of the high-heeled shoes she was wearing. Her dress hung neatly over her hips; her stockings were dark, almost rust-coloured, to go with the dress. She was stylish all right, in an unmistakably self-assured, somewhat overdone, middle-aged fashion.

Not his style, at all. Another generation's.

Foxborough was the nearer of the two to him. My friend went over and stood firmly at the poet's elbow until the man he was talking to, a loose-lipped, bow-tie-wearer, apparently a BBC colleague, finally gave ground.

'I must go now. It's – '

'You mustn't go.' Even amid the noise of the party, or what was left of it, the tone of his voice was remote and stern. As if in some high-domed building, a multitude of ironic echoes seemed to lurk within it. 'You can't go until we've had a chat.'

With some effort, his guest smiled. 'What about?'

'Well, the interview I haven't given you, for one thing.'

Their eyes met. Foxborough's irises might have been composed of a dark, fractured material, aggregated at unimaginable pressure. But the nakedness of his once-hidden face also made

41

him appear vulnerable, or at any rate more youthful than before. He had not always been the age he was now, and it somehow showed in his cheek-bones especially: they were so fine, and stood out at such a wide angle from one another.

'Shall we set it up again?'

'I have no objection.'

*

That had been Diana's phrase about her husband's invitation to him. She had no objection. He has no objection. They have no objection.

He said: 'I have no objection either.'

'Good. Then let's arrange it.'

'Now?'

'Why not?'

Foxborough pulled a small flat diary out of his pocket, and began paging through it.

It has to figure as a sign of the young man's naïveté, his ignorance of the world in general and of writers in particular, that until then it had not occurred to him that Foxborough might be as eager to be interviewed as he himself had once been to interview him. Yet here was the evidence of it: off-hand, fine-skinned, high-toned Foxborough, who had been writing and publishing for decades, whose poems were read and admired by a few chosen spirits as far afield as Cape Town, was paging through his diary, pencil in hand, eagerly looking for a date that would suit them both. And all for an appearance in some student magazine nobody would ever see!

It was pathetic. It was as pathetic as being a cuckold or a complaisant husband (if either was what he was).

*

But they did not make the date then, Foxborough's eagerness to do so notwithstanding. They were interrupted by a stout, floridly drunken man who took Foxborough by the arm, shouting, 'Rodney! Rodney! Listen to this!' and at once fell into a stunned, amnesiac silence.

Rotund and bespectacled, shorter than Foxborough, his brown hair in a quiff, he swayed backwards and forwards, seeming to expend as much effort in breathing as in remaining upright. The

42

knot of his tie, like a hangman's noose, had climbed round the side of his neck; as a result, one point of the collar stuck out horizontally.

'Rodney – ' he tried again, almost *sotto voce*, and some spittle gathered sadly in the corner of his mouth and slowly began to course downhill, like a tear.

Foxborough's many years in the BBC had evidently taught him patience in dealing with drunks. He smiled encouragingly at his guest, who was still swaying silently before him. The man came to rest. Then, with an intent expression and a curious scraping sound from his shoes, he plunged straight forward, like a diver, aiming himself directly at the floor.

As he went down, his carcass-like weight almost took with it the two men in front of him. They staggered, involuntarily breaking his fall, but they could not prevent it.

The noise produced a moment's silence in the room. It was followed by some gasps and exclamations, and a general movement towards the fallen man.

'He's just passed out,' Foxborough said calmly, gazing down.

The man remained motionless where he had dropped. Twisted to one side, he lay there almost like a hunting trophy of some kind. Foxborough, standing above him, might have been waiting for a celebratory photograph to be taken.

'There's nothing to worry about,' Foxborough said after a seemingly reflective pause.

With the help of a few volunteers the casualty was raised to his feet, more or less, and half-carried, half-dragged to a room in the front of the house. There he was laid down on a couch. His shoes were taken off, his collar and belt undone, his tie hung over the back of a chair. By now he had recovered consciousness of a kind. Gulping, trying to struggle upright, he was brokenly uttering apologetic and facetious phrases: 'Very sorry . . . not like me . . . take no notice . . . spoil your party . . . kiss me, Hardy . . .' and so forth.

Diana, who had come into the room, made no attempt to soothe him. 'I'll go and get a basin,' she said, after silently assessing his condition from a couple of paces away. 'Better safe than sorry.' A little later she returned with a blanket, a china bowl, and some newspaper in her hand. The others withdrew while Diana covered the man, who had now fallen silent; she placed the newspaper and the bowl on the floor, as close to his head as she could get them. 'That's that,' she announced when she came out of the room, closing the door behind her.

'As long as he's still breathing,' someone said.

'Oh, he's breathing all right,' she answered, making no attempt to hide the irritation in her voice.

*

For the sake of the record it should be mentioned that the central figure in that little drama was a Member of Parliament (Labour) who was subsequently to become a minister, and eventually a member of the Cabinet. Many years later, also at a private party, I had the opportunity of seeing him perform in rather similar fashion. Just a few months after that, I was to read in the papers that he had collapsed and died in an aeroplane taking him to what was described as an important international conference.

By then Diana too was dead. So was my friend. Only Foxborough, who could hardly have been aware that I knew what had happened in his living-room decades before, was able to share those headlines with me.

*

How long ago all this took place! Imagine, there were no word processors in those days. I could not then have been doing what I am now. The hollow, galloping sound made by fingers on computer keyboards, as of little ponies exercising over hard ground, was simply never heard in the land.

There was much else they were deprived of, in that primitive decade. No fax machines, no colour television, no cash cards for withdrawing money from the bank (no Mastercard! no Visa!), no satellites, no STD. There were many fewer cars in the streets of London; fewer black and brown people in them too. Women swore less in public. Fashions in typography and clothing and furniture were much different from what they were subsequently going to be, from what they are now; and there was not a soul who knew where the differences were to

44

lie. There were no motorways. Factories and warehouses of corrugated aluminium were not to be seen on the outskirts of cities, and no office blocks of glass and plastic had been built within them.

On the other hand, giant brick cinemas were still standing in every town and city in the country. Money was counted in pounds, shillings and pence. Annual salaries of members of the professional classes seldom exceeded four figures. Almost all the aeroplanes in the sky were still tugged forwards, with a visibly effortful motion, by propellers. The war in Korea was not all that long over. The invasions of Hungary by the Soviets and of the Suez area by Britain and France were shortly to come. Stalin was dead but the labour camps in the Soviet Union had not begun to disgorge their prisoners. Over much of Africa the whole paraphernalia of empire was intact. In hot little bush-stations young and middle-aged men out of England and Scotland still solemnly served as district commissioners, assistant district commissioners, medical officers, policemen and the rest.

As you see, I have done my 'research': mostly by watching old films and television programmes. But none of what has just been said really conveys, even to me, the difference which matters most and is hardest to comprehend. It is not just that so many who were alive then are now dead. If they were all dead perhaps the period might seem less strange than it does. Then it would belong securely to history; we would have in common with it only that which knows nothing of any of us, neither of the living nor of the dead – stones, buildings, trees, and so forth.

No, it is the overlap among people which puzzles one most: the secret, inexorable exchange of roles which was taking place then, has always taken place, is taking place now: to such utterly devastating effect and to no effect at all. The children whom the Foxboroughs' guests had left at home in the care of babysitters are themselves now parents and grandparents, some of whom carry the burden of tending for their excessively long-lived elders. A mile away from the Foxboroughs' party, women from another generation to those now in labour were in the delivery rooms of

King's College hospital; other men were driving the taxi-cabs
outside; other footballers were being bought and sold; other
stars were singing their songs; other politicians were then flying
to international meetings . . .

None of those alive then who are alive now occupy the
positions they formerly did. Most of those alive today had
not yet been born. Yet every post, from Prime Minister to
vagrant on the floor of Euston Station, was already filled; all
that had to be done was being done; everything it was possible
for people to feel, was felt.

*

Enter into that living-room, as if on cue, Terence Foxborough
and his schoolmate Patrick.

From the threshold Terence announces, after surveying them
carefully, that his parents' friends are just what he had expected
them to be: 'the halt, the aged, the maimed, the blind, the lame'.
That was why he and Patrick had stayed away from the party.
Now they have come in to 'mop up'.

The delivery of this carefully rehearsed speech safely accomplished, Terence goes on to mutter awkward, polite greetings to
various old friends of the family. Patrick, by contrast, keeps his
head and eyes down throughout, as if to hide his humiliatingly
inflamed and pimpled chin. 'Mopping up' takes the form of the
two boys going to the table on which the food has been put out
and loading their plates promiscuously with whatever happens
still to be available: rice, chicken, prawns, salads, bread rolls,
cheeses. With the world-weary air appropriate to the action
– though not without a nervous glance in the direction of
Terence's parents – they also help themselves to a large glass
of wine apiece, and put a bottle of wine on the floor between
them, for future reference. In chairs placed side by side in the
bay window, they settle down to their eating.

There my friend (nearer to them in age than anyone else
in the room) tells them about the excitement they have just
missed. They are amused and conscientiously unimpressed by his
account of the incident; it is the kind of thing, their expressions
suggest, which is all too familiar to them. His tale finished, he
asks them what they intend doing when they leave school. Their

46

answers interest him not at all. But he cannot take his eyes off Terence. It is almost uncanny for him to see Diana's lips and her full eyes rearranged, reduced, and magically rejuvenated in another's face. The boy's whole face is smaller and thinner (and so much younger!) than hers; but perhaps at his age Diana too had soft, light brown hair, and slight shoulders, and a thin neck; perhaps the back of her hands had looked as delicate and thin-skinned as Terence's, and had the same veins showing through.

It is not true that she was strange to him; not true at all! How could he have thought it? Look with what intimacy he knows the face and hands of this youth, whom he has never seen before. It makes him want to weep and exult at the same time, that he should know them so well, and in so secret a fashion.

As for Terence's strained air of superiority; and, so much at odds with the manner he affects, the beseeching look of his eyes and their fugitive movements (could he be unconsciously affected by the intensity with which the stranger is looking at him?); and the hard, busy bunchings that come and go at the hinges of his jaws as he chews his food; and his disproportionately large schoolboy feet, in creased and down-at-heel black shoes planted on the carpet – these presumably are all his own; they are what he is making of himself.

*

Foxborough *père*, accompanied by another guest, now joins the group: first by standing above it and then by pulling up a chair. The presence of his father at once silences Terence. Patrick, who has taken off his jacket to reveal a white shirt buttoned tightly at his negligible wrists, sips hastily at his wine-glass, as if afraid it might be taken from him. Plainly, if he could think of something to say, he would say it. My friend, who feels that he is overstaying his welcome, especially as he had formally announced himself to be on his way out some time ago, is more or less in the same plight. The only one at his ease, apparently, is Foxborough, who breathes in deeply and exhales, and then drinks without haste from the glass of whisky and water in his hand: a tired host at the end

47

of a party. By this time just about half a dozen people are left in the room.

Patrick has at last thought of something to say. 'It must have been a big decision to shave off your beard,' he suggests, and then giggles to show that he means no offence.

'It grew on an impulse and came off on an impulse,' Foxborough answers politely but obscurely, as if the will of the beard had had nothing to do with his own.

These inane remarks unaccountably irk my friend. Not least when he becomes aware that his hand has half-guiltily stolen up to his moustache, and that Foxborough, who is smiling faintly, has seen it do so.

'I was just on my way out,' he says, getting to his feet. 'I must go and say goodnight to Mrs Foxborough.'

'Diana, Diana,' Foxborough murmurs, by way of social instruction.

Their eyes meet again and stay locked together, as if each is daring the other to break off or to continue.

'And do we – er – do you – still want us to fix up that date we were talking about – ?'

'Oh Lord,' Foxborough says, his former eagerness quite gone. 'I honestly don't think I've got the energy to arrange anything now. Why don't you give me a ring soon – in a few days? You can get me at the BBC or here, in the evenings. By that time I'll be coherent again. I hope.'

'Yes, I'll do that.'

That is what my friend says. Internally he vows that he will see this cold fish of an Englishman frying in hell first. Passing through his mind, the phrase actually produces in hallucinatory fashion the image of a fish-and-chip man thrusting a wire basket of fish-segments into a bin of frying oil; he even seems to hear the joyful shriek and sizzle that follows: all of it in some anonymous, infernal, steam-grimed interior.

And this while smiling still at the man beneath him.

*

Now to Diana. He finds her alone in the kitchen, standing amid a silent disorder of plates and bottles, cutlery, paper napkins, pans rimmed with congealed rice. On the floor are two red

48

rubbish-bins, like a pair of force-fed dwarfs, their mouths agape, unable to swallow what has been crammed into them.

He takes her hand. It is adorned with several rings and a few freckles, as well as some drops of water hanging from it. He kisses the very tips of her fingers. With her free hand she lightly touches the back of his neck.

'Wet,' she says apologetically.

'I've been talking to Terence. He looks a lot like you. It's strange. He doesn't look like his father at all.'

'Rodney?' Looking down at the sink she makes a vague movement towards it. 'Rodney wouldn't want anybody to look like him. Rodney's one of a kind.'

'What's that supposed to mean?'

Before she can answer he seizes her by the wrist. 'Why *me*? What were you up to?'

Her answer brings with it a movement of her head and a glint of unadmitted mirth in her eyes: something he has seen there before.

'I wanted to give you a surprise. I didn't know how else to do it.'

The mirth now touches the corner of her lips. She might almost be talking to a child. 'A nice surprise, I mean. A happy surprise.'

He cannot speak. Her expression changes. She no longer looks at him, but at one of the rubbish-bins beneath her. Sombrely, like someone counting off a litany of medieval sins, she says, 'Also desire, of course. Vanity. Mischief. Compassion.'

'Compassion?'

She looks at him again. His fingers are still clenched around her wrist; he must be hurting her, but she has made no movement to disengage it from his grasp.

'Yes, I did feel sorry for you. You wanted it so badly.'

'Me? Nothing was further from my mind! Not until you put it there – '

'Maybe. But you were full of wanting, all the same. Bursting with it. Staring at me with it.'

Patrick comes into the kitchen behind him. 'Can I have a cloth? Something's been spilt on the carpet.'

49

Could he have seen their hands abruptly parting from each other?

With only the tiniest, enforced expulsion of breath, Diana asks, 'What's been spilt?'

'Some wine.'

'Red or white?'

'Red.'

'It would be!'

She moistens a sponge, picks up a container of salt, and starts to make her way into the living-room.

Once again she has become the busy hostess and housewife, the woman given over to trivial, fateful responsibilities. Patrick has gone ahead of her. At the door she turns and says to him, 'Also, I like you. I thought you were nice. I still do.'

Alone in the kitchen, he is left staring like a madman into the cluttered sink, seemingly hypnotised by an upturned aluminium colander. Inside it white worms of spaghetti are making their nests.

Then he rouses himself and goes to look for his coat. No one sees him leave the house. He takes a bus to Kennington and then the tube to Liverpool Street, as he had done the last time. Again he rides in the train back to Cambridge. Again he leans his head against the carriage window; he gazes into the turbid light and darkness beyond, skimmed always by the reflection the train carries with it. Unknown commuter stations fling wide their spectral arms, and flee. Shattered greenhouses rise out of a waste of mud. Car headlights reach forward between reeling houses, they run with the train, turn away, shrink to a receding ruby dot.

*

Whirled past all of it unresistingly, he was filled with a dread which was always to be associated in his mind with that particular journey. Everything out there appeared commonplace and yet impenetrable, transformed in sinister fashion; and he, the onlooker, seeing it rush by, knew himself to be lost! Doomed!

A few hours later he condemned the anguish he had felt then as melodramatic and hysterical. Years later he marvelled at his own prescience; as well as at its self-centredness.

SIX

When he was away from Diana he found it extraordinarily difficult to remember her. This notwithstanding the intensity with which he would gaze at her, or pore over her, when they were together. He studied her as if she were a piece of writing or a mathematical formula he had to commit to memory. Any turn of her head or arm, any inflection of her voice, could seem to him not merely a part of her but the instantaneous, irreplaceable expression of all she was and ever had been. Yet the more he struggled subsequently to recall such a moment, to re-create some strong, convincing image of her in his mind, the more certain he was to fail.

It was tantalising, and worse than that; it fed his obsession with her. Glimpses of her only were vouchsafed to him, fragments emerging from mist and blankness. Her face especially eluded him. He could remember moments of it (so to speak): the shadows under her eyes, it might be – shadows which were sometimes brownish in hue, sometimes almost mauve, and which had within them small curved wrinkles that mimed or followed exactly the curve of the eye itself. But her face, the whole being which manifested itself in her face, he could not recover. The instant his back was turned she began to dissipate, to be lost to him. A few hundred yards could render her both unforgotten and yet unreal. Unreal and therefore impossible to forget.

It was almost as if she were playing some kind of trick on him.

As a result he was overwhelmed, whenever he saw her, by the simple recognition of her reality, by the rediscovered fullness of her presence. His inner exclamation, in that first moment, was not, 'Oh, there she is!' but something odder, more relieved and more surprised: 'Oh, *that's* what she's like!' Or even, 'Of course! Look, that's her!'

She used only powder and lipstick, both quite copiously; nothing else, apart from the golden dye she inflicted on her hair; no creams; never any perfume. Yet when he tore open a letter from her it seemed to fill the room with her fragrance; all the more precious because it was so faint. He could smell it on his fingertips as well as on the paper, which he would bring to his nostrils over and over again, astonished that such faintness could have so much power over him. He could never mistake the smell for any other in the world. And then that testimony to her reality, even in her absence, would fade and dissipate too, and he would be left at a loss, feeling that he had nothing of her within himself to sustain him during her absence.

*

AN EXCHANGE OF LETTERS
(in the Chinese manner)

(1)

The moon rises as it has to, enlarged, enflamed, engorged,
 with the day's heat.
Windows are open, doors too. Barefoot weather.
Outside, black leaves that lift their heads and hiss,
 then fall silent.
And in my heart – you, you, you.

Why you? I go to town; the train is full of women.
I walk in the street; they pass on every side.
It is clear to me, then, that randomness reigns.
Yet here I sit, still wishing you were with me now;
Or that we had never met;
Or that you had not been born for me to love.

For nothing else.

Never anything else.

Your letter was brought to me by a man in a peaked cap.
He had a sallow skin; it shone in the heat.
I offered him a drink of water but he refused it.
He said he had many other letters to deliver.

*

Pretty soon he had worked out a rationale for his feelings about her. Yes, he was obsessed with her. Yes, it was absurd and incongruous, given the difference in age between them. No, there was no 'future' in the relationship; how could there be? She would grow old – really old; he would soon (months ahead? a year ahead? who could tell?) come into his full manhood; he would fall away from her, and she from him. He knew it. She knew it.

No, he did not mind that there was no future in their relationship. On the contrary. Its having no future was vital to it. That was exactly why he could afford to give himself over to it. It was a stage, a phase, a part of his growing up, 'finding himself' in this new-old country. Indeed, he positively looked forward now to being able to look back on the affair; he rehearsed the emotions he would be sure to feel then: sadness and tenderness chiefly (tenderness towards himself too), but also amusement, gratitude for a sophistication and an understanding of women he could have acquired nowhere else and from no one else. Emotions such as these would suit very well the mature man he would by then have become. He would never forget how much he owed to her; how much he had learned from her.

Yes – no – yes – there was nothing *wrong* with his being in love with a woman nearly twice his age, the mother of a boy almost as old as himself, the wife of another man (who happened, moreover, to be a famous poet). Nothing in the world wrong with it. Blank, boring Bloemfontein, sprawling about on the veld, the sun raging in the middle of its ashen sky, might have thought it wrong or sick; but Bloemfontein did not know about such things; or knew about them only to snigger or guffaw or shake its narrow head at them. That what he was doing might be traditional, customary, *French*, for God's sake;

that in Diana's arms he might be the hero of a novel, a young man from the provinces learning through passion and pain and, yes, through incongruity too, what he could not have learned in any other fashion, or from any other woman than this one – none of this Bloemfontein could be expected to understand.

He was simply not going to let go; that was the truth. Not until it had, alas, become apparent to them both that the time for letting go and looking sadly back had at last come.

How he looked forward to those backward glances! With what rueful romantic longing they were (in advance) infused!

*

And she? Are we to see her only as he saw her? Must he always get in the way of our view of her?

I am afraid he does (for the most part). Obviously, being the one who brought the tale to me he will always have that advantage – if it is an advantage – over her.

But there is another reason why escaping from him and his view of her is so difficult. He has made it so: as if deliberately. Whatever character or motives I or anyone else might wish to ascribe to her, whatever impulses we might choose to impute to her, he has pre-empted us. At least in one or another of his moods he has done so.

Try to think of her as the mature, wise, sensuous, life-loving woman, with so much to give and so great a readiness to receive that no one man could ever satisfy her – and there you will find him, my friend, thinking those very thoughts. Call her a shallow bitch, an habitual liar, a ballbreaker – and guess who will have preceded you there? Think of her as a pathetic creature on whom middle-age, with all its terrors, has closed, and who is trying desperately to prove to herself that she can still look forward to change and excitement in her life; that she still has the power to attract men – and there he is once again, focussing on the poor woman a gaze as stony as he can make it. Or what about Diana as the victim of a helpless infatuation with a man half her age, at war with her own judgement and self-respect: the Phaedra of Herne Hill or East Dulwich, no less? Or as an unwitting victim of another kind: one tied to an older man who is cleverer and more powerful than herself, in whose shadow she has always lived and against whom she is struggling to get the only form of revenge she can?

Everywhere you go, you will find that someone else – Adrian Bester, our hero or coxcomb – has been there already. And there is to be no getting past him or around him by trying to imagine Diana divested of him, untroubled by any thought of him, as she had been before he had met her. Of that Diana, or of an earlier Diana still, of the innocent, ignorant, virginal young woman she had once been, the Diana of the small, shiny, black-and-white snapshots he begged off her, which showed her with her hair longer or shorter than he had ever seen it, or piled up in two preposterous horns above her forehead in the fashion of the day; or Diana dressed in an antiquated bathing costume, with her bare knees shyly pressed together; or laughing in somebody's garden, while a baldheaded, pipe-smoking, long-dead father looks on – that Diana, the ever-unattainable one, living a life of her own before he had even been born, Diana the schoolgirl who had once sat in a desk and wondered vaguely what she would do with her life, what men she would meet, what countries she would live in – she above all others became the object of the poor man's obsession.

*

Ironically enough, he had let himself into this labyrinth by trying to break out of it. He had decided to confront her, to make a clean breast of how much he had found himself thinking about her after that party, with its final exchanges between them in the kitchen. He was determined to clear the air, to get the whole thing out into the open, to get it out of his system . . .

That had been his plan and those had been the phrases with which he had encouraged himself beforehand. She had spoken of his beggingly 'wanting' her when he himself had had no inkling that this desire was harboured in his heart or could be read on his face. Very well then! Let her see how he behaved and what he could do when he was ready to acknowledge such a need;

and then, once for all, let her see how resolutely he could put it behind him.

Several weeks after the party, therefore, he sought her out in the last place where she might have expected him to appear. In order to find her there he had been forced to do some detective work, since all he knew about the place he was seeking was that it was 'near' the Foxboroughs' address, somewhere in Herne Hill. This had meant going about the area on successive Fridays (Saturdays were no good; he knew she did not work then), with his *A–Z London* atlas in his hand and in his pocket a list of local hardware stores he had copied from a South London business directory.

What a way to spend one's Fridays! What a way to seek out the wife of one of England's well-known poets! It irritated him beyond measure to think that she could *afford* to work in a hardware shop without any loss of self-esteem. That was how secure she felt herself to be. His mother, who had struggled to become a primary-school teacher in a bare, white-plastered Bloemfontein school, fronted with coarse turf and beds of cannas, ringed with a red cement stoep and roofed in corrugated iron, could never have done it; would never have done it.

Perhaps the same effortless assumption of superiority had been at work when Diana had taken him into her arms, into herself, on the floor of her living-room. A Boer! A hungry, self-revealing nobody who had had the impudence to admire her husband's poems, and fancied himself as a sensitive soul, therefore!

Compassion, was it, that she had felt for him?

*

The shop was one of a terrace of about half a dozen, with low windows and flats above them. A similar terrace faced it across a busy roadway. At a distance of about thirty yards, slanting over the traffic, was a high-sided railway bridge. Occasionally this bridge shook and produced obscure sounds, at once metallic and intestinal, but the trains passing inside it could never be seen.

She was standing behind a glass-topped counter. He had not

been in touch with her since the party. He had been determined that she should not know that he was looking for her. That was why he had made none of his enquiries by telephone. It was imperative to take her by surprise. The look on her face told him how well he had succeeded.

While she still gaped at him, he took out of his pocket the list of shop names and addresses he had been carrying and presented it to her. More than half the names on it had already been scored through in his search for her. She studied the list intently. Standing there he might indeed have been a shopper who had come looking for a number of items of which he had made a careful note; and she the conscientious assistant checking whether or not the goods were in stock.

'You're mad!' she said finally, looking up from the list.

He did not deny it. On the contrary, he was proud of having forced her to say it.

'Is there anywhere we can go and talk?'

'I'm working . . .'

He jerked his head towards the door through which he had come in. 'Is that your boss?'

'Yes.'

Leaving her, he went over to the man behind the counter on the other side of the shop, who had been eyeing them both suspiciously. 'Excuse me,' he said in his best Timpkins-trained voice, 'can I ask a favour of you? Could Mrs Foxborough come out with me for . . . just a half-hour or so. I'm her – her – nephew from South Africa, and I'm passing through, and I don't know when I'll have another chance of seeing her.'

Diana's boss wore a shiny blue shopcoat on his slight frame, and what was intended to be a ferocious moustache on his narrow face. The brown flourish of it filled his upper lip entirely and crawled up his cheeks on both sides. But his brow was anxiously wrinkled and his doggy eyes were mild. Silent, undecided, smelling a rat, his gaze went from the one to the other of them.

'She'll make it up during her lunch-hour.'

'Oh yes,' Diana assured him, coming up from behind. 'I promise you.'

*

The one unusual thing about the shops in that terrace was that there was a wig-maker among them. A large sign said so. In its window were displayed some nightmarishly featureless, bald, bust-like dummies, awaiting their wigs. The very next day he could remember vividly the row of head-shapes standing there; and the coarsely woven, gingerish material in which they were covered. But of Diana herself at his side there remained only the knowledge that she had been with him. Her full, living presence eluded him again.

*

They came to a park. It had a pond and some huts behind fences of wooden stakes and wire. Among the shrubs small birds scuffled and wheezed. Sticky-looking waxen buds hung down from bare branches of horse-chestnuts; at angles, beyond the trees, spaces of turf stretched away. Intermittently the sun emerged and disappeared in a lofty, cloudy sky: bringing or wiping out, with equal indifference, pale shadows. It was mid-week, mid-morning, mid-school term; the park was empty.

He had rehearsed thoroughly what he was going to say. To his surprise he not only remembered the phrases he had devised, but brought them out more or less in the order he had intended to. She helped him by not interrupting. Indeed she hardly looked at him. Nor did he look at her. He saw her feet in their pointed leather shoes, and heard the noise they made on the asphalt path. She was wearing pale stockings, and a loose woollen overcoat. Its hem moved against her legs.

He told her that he still did not know why she had made love to him the afternoon he had come to the house. That was all right. He had heard what she had said to him at the party, but he did not know how much of it he should believe. That was also all right. He did not know why he had done what he had, either, except that the opportunity had been given to him and he would have thought himself a coward and a weakling if he had not taken it. He was not making excuses for himself; nor was he making any claim on her. He could not make a claim

58

on her. She was married. She was a mother. She was too old for him; he was too young for her. The gulfs between them, all the differences in their circumstances, could not be bridged.

That was all right too. He had come to tell her simply that he had been thinking of her ever since the night of the party. The thought of her had a power over him he did not understand. He would not call it love. He did not know what it should be called. He wanted her to be aware of it: that was all. Until he had told her about it he would not be free of it. Not speaking to her was the one intolerable thing. He had to get it off his chest. To get it into the open and hence out of his system. Now he had done it. It was over. It would not matter now if they never saw each other again. It would be better for them both if they did not.

They were back at the gate of the park. It opened directly on the road. Every car that went by seemed to give a separate, scornful buffet to the little space of air they shared.

'You see,' he said, 'you'll be back at work before the half-hour is up,' and turned and walked away in the opposite direction from the one she would have taken. He did not expect to see her again.

*

Well, she followed him. Easy to say (in retrospect) that she was bound to do it. Not so easy for her to do, however.

She promised him nothing. She did not even undertake to see him again. She said only, staring fixedly at his chest, no higher, 'If we do meet again, you must swear to me that you'll never let Rodney know.'

'If that's how you want it,' he answered readily enough.

He was astonished that she had followed him. It was a submission of some kind; it had to be. That was all he noticed, for the moment.

Then he asked, as if the question were distant from them both: 'Would he mind that much?'

She responded fiercely: '*I* would mind.'

They parted without making any definite arrangement to meet each other again. She would not let him do it. 'Later, later,' she said, when he made an attempt to speak of it. Her eyes still evaded his.

59

He put his hand on top of her head, on her stiff hair, as if it were something on which an oath could be taken. The words that broke out of him sounded almost enraged. 'I need you! I need you!'

She made no response. It was for her now to turn her back on him, for him to stand on the pavement and watch her go.

*

Two points.

First. It would be wrong to suppose that because he had rehearsed his speech, and because it came out just as he had wished it to, it must therefore have lost its warmth. Not at all. His own words moved him even more, as he said them, than they would have if he had had to make them up on the spot. He did not have to think about them. They were ready for him. All he had to do was to inhabit them.

Second: the fact that his speech had quite the opposite effect from what he had intended actually gave him a sense of inner peace, even of fulfilment, which he had not known since the night of the party. Ending the doubt as to whether or not there *was* a relationship between them came as something of a relief. He could relax now; relax into his obsession with her, however paradoxical that might sound. They had both acknowledged that what they had done together was to have consequences for them both, even if they could not imagine what these might be.

SEVEN

The next time they met was in a room in a hotel near the Cromwell Road.

He had never set up an assignation of this kind before; among its other excitements, therefore, it was charged with a sense of mystery of which he felt himself to be not the least mysterious part. Even that district of London, with its grim, ornate buildings and lurching traffic, was one he barely knew. Outside the hotel was a tree-filled square where pedestrians went by, bent on their ordinary weekday business. Another mystery, there, each one of them! The branches of the plane trees in the square moved restlessly, as if the tiny, tawny leaves struggling to break out of them were an itch, an irritation of some kind; there was even a taint of blood in their hue. Barely a week later they would spring free, into a sudden green; another few weeks and they would have made of themselves an unfamiliar weight for the breeze to lift, a new element among all the others of which the city was composed.

He lay on the bed which he would soon be sharing with Diana, wondering at how little and how much he knew of her. Doubtless she had entered many hotel rooms like this one, in similar circumstances; perhaps during the war, too, in a time of bombs and darkness, of fears and dislocations unimaginable to him. His mind grew dim at the thought of it. That she should have been through the war, and he had not, in whatever form it had taken for her, whatever she had seen and felt . . .

Then, with a hurried knock on the door, Diana came in. There she was, all of her, in the present, exactly as he had struggled so hard and so unsuccessfully to remember her. Except that she was wearing soft, crumpled, black boots, zipped up at the side and reaching to just below her knee, which he had never seen before.

The smell of leather and nylon filled his nostrils as he knelt down to undo them. This smell was also new; also hers, for ever.

*

They met several times in that hotel, or others like it. After the first occasion Diana insisted on paying her share of the cost, and he was happy to let her do so – though he pointed out that he got more out of the deal than she did. For she could never stay more than a couple of hours, whereas he would usually stay overnight too.

Sometimes, after Diana had got out of bed, he simply lay where he was, with his eyes closed, luxuriating in a darkness which for him was unlike any other, for it was filled with the soothing, secretive noises made by her garments as she picked them up and donned them, one by one. Little gasps they uttered; slithers, rustles, flicks and bites, sighs, soft creaks, the sudden, kittenlike mew of a zip. Also there were the gentle footsteps with which these sounds were interspersed; and the audible pout with which she applied lipstick to her lips; and the severe, dry busyness of hairbrushing at the very end.

That was one pleasure, or series of pleasures; another was to open his eyes and to watch her wrapping her body away from him, concealing from others everything it had revealed to him. He loved to see its clumsy hangings forward and wrinklings beneath; for reasons he could not begin to understand, he loved also the marks on it of what it had been through – of having given birth, of having been used, known to others.

Yet there was pleasure, too, in dressing while she dressed, and then going downstairs and drinking a cup of coffee with her, in the hotel or in some place just outside it, and seeing her off into the busy street. They kissed briefly when they parted, nothing more; in public they did not so much as hold hands, though they looked into one another's eyes with the unmistakable gaze of lovers.

In his heart he felt a secret, guilty relief that this show of restraint had been agreed between them, without a word having been said on either side. No one who saw them was going to be provoked to mirth or prurient speculation about the difference of age between them.

*

Afterwards, for him, came the more doubtful pleasures of memory: the usual, musing wonder as to why he could remember so vividly the pattern of a wallpaper, say, or of the pipes running down some brick back-wall, and the vaguely drifting skies above, while Diana herself always succeeded in remaining elusive to the eye of memory.

*

And elusive not only to the eye of memory, either. She held him, hugged him, cried out to him, sucked in his breath, her tongue rested limply against his, as if it had lost its life in his mouth or hers, she seemed to begrudge him nothing; and at the same time, the more he saw her, the more familiar she became to him, the better he understood what she responded to, so the less, it seemed to him, he really knew who or what she was. It was as if he could do what he liked with her body; but in the spirit she remained impenetrable to him. The frustration of it sometimes made him frantic. No wonder he could never remember her body as he wished to, once he was away from her, when the soul of it was denied him!

He wanted to *know* – but could not say even to himself what it was that he wanted to know. (Other than everything.) He wanted to *understand* – and was baffled to think what sort of understanding he craved, what its object might be. Within him, full-grown yet always changing, as irrational as it was stubborn, there was a conviction that there must be a way of prising out of her some set of words which would make her wholly comprehensible to him; and thus make him comprehensible to himself. There had to be an explanation, several explanations, why he loved Diana as he did, and she loved him. There had to be a definition of the kind of love he felt for her, and of the kind of love (so different from his own, it was bound to be) she felt for him.

63

She, she alone, could give him those words: no one else. It stood to reason that in the circumstances he could not expect to find them for himself. To prove it he would once again go through a litany already wearisomely familiar to him. She was so much older than he was. She was better acquainted with the world than he was; especially this ancient, complicated, half-foreign northern world they were living in, which had always been native to her. She had a husband and a child, some famous acquaintances, a life he knew virtually nothing about. What was more she had had all he had found her with for years, for something now approaching twenty years – and God knew what she had been and what she had done before then.

Whereas he had nobody apart from her. He knew only too well what he had been before he had met her. The recollected or imagined emptiness of his own past, in that empty country he came from, furnished with drab streets and great skies and nothing between, now made him ache. As a boy it seemed to him he had always been conscious of insufficiency, of boredom, of wanting more than he had been given. Look at him, cycling along those deserted suburban streets with the sun shining and thin trees casting thin shadows on the pavements! As a student too, in Cape Town, there had always been something hollow even about the pleasures he had experienced. He had loved the smell of the sea there, so novel to him after his upcountry childhood, and the long twilights, also novel, and Table Mountain parked improbably above the city – half-animal; half-spaceship; all scrub and rock. But he had never known until he was in Diana's arms, or just out of them, what a desolation it had all been; or would one day come to seem.

*

Sometimes he was sure that the words he wanted Diana to speak would give their love a solidity and depth it did not now have; it would be released from the doubt and guilt, the shame and disproportion, which constantly threatened it. At other times he looked to those same words, if only they could be found, not to set their love free, but to do the exact opposite: to set them free of it. Once they had been spoken, and his motives and hers had been rendered conscious to them both, they would no longer be bound to one another; then, whether with pain or not, they would be able to bring the affair to the end which had always awaited it.

*

In effect he was never to abandon the search for those words. Long after her death – indeed until the day of his own death – he was still searching for them: trying out this combination and that, this explanation and that, this mode of expurgation or that.

He was never to find them. As the victim or beneficiary of so many of his attempts, I suspect that they were nowhere to be found. So far my experience tells me that words seem to be much better at entrapping us in our obsessions than they ever are at releasing us from them.

*

All this preoccupation with words, on his side at least; and never a word spoken between them about subjects neither could forget. Silence on her side about her husband, about her son, about the future of their relationship. Silence on his side about the misgivings and frustrations that had begun to torment him. He would never have thought it possible, beforehand.

The very first time he began to say something about her husband, she held up a warning, silencing finger: a gesture all the more decisive for the silence in which it was made.

'What – ?'

Before he could say more, she just shook that upraised finger, her gaze fixed severely on him.

'So what are we allowed to talk about?' he asked.

'Nothing very much,' she answered.

'For ever?'

'For as long as we can.'

Like the interdiction on any exchange of caresses in public, the ban actually gave an added zest to their meetings. It made them seem even more secretive and carnal than they already were. In any case, talking about 'nothing very much' came easily to them. It always had. She told him about giving up her job in the hardware shop: 'The man's a twerp' – her explanation. He told her about getting into the First Eleven of the college

65

cricket team: 'They've got no one else' – his explanation. She told him what she liked about his face. 'It's kind of nice and round.' He explained what he liked about hers. 'Kind of nice and wrinkled' – whereupon there followed pinches and blows, and then what often follows these, between lovers. He talked about the essays he was writing for his tutor. She about why she enjoyed selling things. 'You meet people. You talk to them about what they want. You see them making up their minds. If they go away happy with what they've bought, you feel good about it. Anyone can understand that. And if you find something they haven't been able to get elsewhere, or suggest something they haven't thought of for a particular purpose – then that's good too.'

'I care too much about obliging people,' she added, in a tone which would have been wistful if she had not adopted a bogus American accent to go with it.

In her last life, she told him, she had been an old pedlar-woman ('You know – fat'), selling stuff from a basket. Then they had burned her for a witch. That had been a long time ago.

'Now,' she said, 'I must stop messing about with all these stupid jobs.' She laughed suddenly, recollecting that her boss in the hardware shop had given her a bradawl, of all improbable things, as a farewell present. It was his phallic, farewell symbol, twisty at the end. 'I think he liked me, poor man.' Then her expression became grave. 'I must settle down now and look for something that's really got some prospects.'

He was enchanted by this middle-aged woman (wife of a famous poet), who had apparently started and abandoned numerous inconsequential jobs, imagining herself finding employment with 'prospects'. And so seriously too. And yet not seriously at all. She made out of her own puzzlements a comedy which depended on a constant uncertainty – in herself as much as in her listener – as to whether or not she meant to be funny.

He said to her: 'If you hadn't been working in that hardware shop, we wouldn't be here today. You remember? That's what set us off.'

'What?' she answered blankly. 'Was it? How?'

'You don't remember?' he cried, remembering only too vividly his own callow surprise at hearing what she did, and everything that had followed from it.

'No,' she said. 'I don't know what you're talking about.'

He stared into her eyes; all he saw in the poignantly imperfect blue-grey of her irises, open to his gaze, was a blank forgetfulness.

*

The pleasures of adultery turned out to be indistinguishable, for him, from its pains; indeed, its pleasures *were* its pains, and vice versa. It was impossible to recognise the separations it enforced, the secrecy it entailed, the deceits and deprivations native to it, from the intensity and even the exultation of surrendering to it.

*

SONG

He thinks of her as she used to be
in years before he knew her.
'Was she with them as she is with me:
or kinder, softer, truer?

'Did she hold them so and kiss them so,
and smile in just that way?
And when she sighed so long ago,
did I hear it – yesterday?

'And were such questions asked of her
by others in their turn?
O what is hidden in the heart of her
that I have still to learn?'

*

Since silence was the rule (her rule), he did not tell her that he had telephoned her husband and renewed the arrangement to interview him. It was from Foxborough himself that she learned of it.

She did not write to complain about this; nor did she leave a message for him at his college suggesting a time when he could phone her, which was how they had often communicated in the past. She was not in the house when he called there with his tape recorder and his prepared questions. She simply failed to turn up at their next appointment.

He did not complain, either. He spent the night alone in the hotel where they had arranged to meet, and returned to Cambridge.

This was a silence of a different kind between them. It was broken, if it was broken at all, only by the sound of Foxborough's voice on his tape. Again and again he jabbed at the clumsy buttons of the old-fashioned, brief-case-like tape recorder; again and again he sent the tape racing back on itself with a hiss and a rattle, or rushed it fast-forward, so that the voices on it, his and Foxborough's, turned into a high-pitched gibber, at once childlike and demonic; he halted it at this moment or that, sometimes catching just what he wanted: Foxborough's voice, curiously flattened in tone by the machine, and yet as full as ever of an abstracted self-assurance, saying something that seemed to be directed not at the readers of OMEGA (whoever the hell they might be), but at him, the interviewer – the man whom the poet, sitting behind his desk, talking into the microphone, had seemed to arraign over and over again with his complicated yet impervious eye.

EIGHT

*This interview took place in Rodney Foxborough's study, on
the first floor of his home in Dulwich, South London. The
room is of modest size; its walls are painted a pleasant, open
beige colour; the woodwork is cream, the ceiling white. One
wall is wholly given over to bookshelves which reach almost to
the ceiling. Throughout the interview the poet sat at his desk,
a multi-drawered, Victorian piece of furniture with a scarred
green leather top. Everything on it was neatly in place. There
are several pictures on the walls, one of them a Sickert which,
Foxborough told me, had been given to him by the artist in
his old age. There are also some small oils by friends from
the Euston Road Group (Coldstream, du Plessis), as well as a
pair of matching charcoal sketches of the poet and his wife by
Colm Tapscott, which hang directly opposite the desk, above
a green-tiled fireplace. One can quite easily imagine the study
as the family bedroom it must once have been. The curved
street outside is a quiet one, occupied by houses like the poet's
own: solidly (not to say stolidly) built, yet decorated with the
childish flourishes typical of the 1880s – Gothic porches; plaster
Corinthian columns dividing the bay windows on the ground
floor; hooped, terracotta ridges along the apex of the slate roofs.*

*Rodney Foxborough (b. 1905) was casually dressed in a
brown sweater and corduroy trousers. He answered the questions put to him briskly enough; so briskly indeed as to suggest
a positive disdain for some of the issues which the interviewer
tried to raise. It must be emphasised, however, that at no time
did he express any reluctance to be interviewed. Far from it.*

*

Mr Foxborough, what do you feel to be the function of the poet in modern society?

To write poems.

And the function of his poems?

To rid him (temporarily) of the desire to write more poetry.

Is that all? Where do readers come in?

Later.

I didn't ask 'when' they come in, but where.

True. But my answer remains the same. Readers have to wait until the thing is finished. Only then – assuming of course that there are of them to be found – does their turn come. One must never forget, in any case, that the overwhelming majority of people are neither readers nor writers of poetry, nor of anything else much, and don't give a damn for either activity.

Who are the poets who have most influenced you?

The usual ones for somebody of my age, I suppose. Plus Lewis Carroll.

Lewis Carroll?

Yes, you know, the man who wrote *Alice in Wonderland*.

Why him, particularly?

I used to read the two *Alice* books constantly when I was a boy. I also liked some of his other nonsense verse: 'The Hunting of the Snark' and so forth. It was my admiration for him that first made me seriously think of becoming a writer. He also made me want to become a mathematician, and a clergyman of the Church of England, and a Fellow of Christ Church, Oxford – just as he was. Alas, I've succeeded in fulfilling only the first of those ambitions, up to a point.

Have you got other unfulfilled ambitions?

Well, one always wants to be a better writer than one actually is. I would have liked to have been a better soldier than I was during my spell as an artillery officer, at the beginning of the war. I would like to be a better father than I am.

In what sense?

Less impatient. I would also like to be a better husband than I am.

How?

Less indifferent.

Do you feel that working in the BBC and elsewhere has interfered with your career as a poet?

I have never had a 'career' as a poet. The BBC makes it possible for me to write poetry. It pays my salary. Also, one is a poet for only so many – or so few – hours in the week. What would I do with the rest of my time, if I did not have a job? Be bored? Write reviews? Think about my reputation? I would far rather be at my desk in the BBC, especially now that I have an administrative job. I enjoy administration. It is always a challenge to find new ways of adjusting the rules to the people – when it's possible; and of adjusting the people to the rules – if they will allow it to be done.

The title of your last volume, 'Bruised to Pleasure', is taken from a line in a poem by W.B. Yeats. In it he expresses the wish that intellectual and aesthetic pursuits did not bring about a loss of spontaneity and physical appetite. He longs for a world in which 'body is not bruised to pleasure soul'. Did you choose this phrase for the title of your book because you feel yourself to have suffered a loss of that kind?

No, not at all. The line suggested to me something quite different. I liked the idea that bruising and being bruised could actually be a source of pleasure. That's why I chose it.

Do you think that is what Yeats meant when he wrote the line?

Probably not. But he can't complain about the way I have chosen to read it, and to use it.

You feel that a poem or story belongs to its readers, rather than to its writer, once it has been made public?

It's as difficult for me to understand the idea of a poem 'belonging' to anyone as the idea of its 'function', which you were talking about earlier. Once a poem has been published it becomes public property. It's rather like . . . I don't know – a park bench, say. Anyone can come and rest his bottom on it. Any dog can come and lift his hind-leg against it. The poet really can't lurk about behind the bushes, like some wretched park-keeper, trying to make sure that the bench is used only for purposes he approves of. Imagine him shouting out, 'No snogging here!

Kindly admire the view: or move along at once!' Nor should any reader or critic try to take on that role. Sometimes one feels that most critics are merely park-keepers *manqué*. There's nothing they would like better than a uniform and a whistle. For myself, I have no hankering for either item of equipment. Of that you can be sure. Perhaps I suffer from an altogether underdeveloped sense of property. I would rather have less of it, in all spheres of life, than too much.

It's been said that you have moved in your verse from a looser, more romantic, sometimes even surrealist style to one which is now rather harsh and bare. Would you agree?

No.

Why not?

I don't like your adjectives.

Is there any other feature of your childhood, apart from your admiration for Lewis Carroll, which you now feel to have been important in helping or compelling you to become a poet?

Oh, almost as far back as I can remember I was always writing something or other. It was no doubt very trying for everyone around me, constantly having me thrust my verses and stories and plays at them. Not to mention my 'essays'. I grew up in the golden age – tinsel age, rather – of the whimsical little essay about nothing at all, written by people whose names now mean nothing at all. So of course I aped the form zealously. My parents submitted to reading these things with a good grace, I must say. And I suppose that even at that age I had managed to get hold of something which was quite important for me, if not for my adult victims. Any beginner wants to produce something like the writers he admires. He doesn't necessarily want to *be* like them, or to feel like them. But he longs to be able to write like them. Or even better: he longs to imagine what it must be like already to have done it. Imagine affecting somebody else, the reader-yet-to-be, as you yourself have been affected by the work of others! What a pleasure for them – as well as for you! Let that be my belated excuse, anyhow, for the stuff I inflicted on my parents.

What did your father do?

He was a barrister who later became a high-court judge.

King's Bench Division, as it was in those days. He was a great, burly man, quite unlike me physically. About six-foot three, and heavy all over. He'd been wounded in the trenches in the First World War, and had a kind of limp or lurch as a result, which somehow made him look even larger than he might otherwise have done. He must have been a fearsome figure on the bench, all rigged up in his robes, and with a wig perched on his outsize head. Unfortunately I never saw him in the role. He forbade my brother and me from going into any court he was appearing in, or presiding over, and we were much too much in awe of him to disobey. Incidentally, neither his size nor his limp prevented him from being an enthusiast for boating and sailing; it was one of the things he and I used to do happily together. Eventually he had to give it up; and I gave it up too, and never really went back to it. Looking back from the age I am now to the age he was then, I must say I admire his pertinacity much more than I was capable of doing as a child.

Did your mother work?

No, she was a mother and a wife. She used to do some charitable work, though, of a genteel kind. For some reason we lived in Devonshire Place, next to Harley Street, among all the medical people – they had flats there, as well as consulting rooms, in those days – and my mother got involved in committee work among the doctors' wives.

Have you tried seriously to write fiction, since the childhood efforts you mentioned a moment ago? Or drama?

Not since I was a schoolboy, no.

Do you read fiction?

No.

Do you go to plays?

As seldom as possible.

What do you do by way of relaxation?

Walk. Womanise. Drink. Do crossword puzzles. Write poems.

What kind of work did you do in Intelligence during the war?

I am not allowed to tell you exactly. I'm still bound to secrecy in the matter. That was work with a 'function', if you like, and very satisfactory it was too.

What are you writing at the moment?
A sonnet sequence.
About?
As it happens, it is about the sending and decoding of signals. I don't suppose I shall be prosecuted under the Official Secrets Act for saying that. It's chiefly about the signals that pass between men and women who are lovers, or who may become lovers, or who have been lovers. But I am also very interested in the kinds of signals that enemies exchange with one another. I learned a great deal during the war on that subject, and on the strange intimacy that exists, that has to exist, between avowed or even undeclared enemies. Of course lovers often feel enmity towards their partners, too, and the not-so-secret messages that pass between them on those terms also interest me greatly.
Is the sequence going well?
Well enough, thank you. I have a lot of material to work on. All literary works are cryptograms of the author's inner life, in one fashion or another. The sonnet form, especially, lends itself to being seen in this way, since it has such strict rules – just as a code does. So I like to think that the form and the content of this particular sequence match one another to an unusually satisfying degree.
You spoke a moment ago about the pleasures of bruising and being bruised. Which of these two pleasures has this interview given you?
Both, I would think. Both.

NINE

There the interview stands, on pages 24–30 of the last issue of OMEGA which was ever to appear. (Volume One, Number Four, published from Nicodemus College, Cambridge.)

I must be the only person in the world to have a complete run of the journal – i.e. all four numbers – in my possession. They have been temporarily loaned to me by the man who was the founder and editor of the whole enterprise: Cronin by name, the friend of my friend. He still treasures these souvenirs of his student days, poor man, and I have promised to return them to him unharmed. He was delighted when I told him that I was curious to look through the copies of the journal; so delighted that, to my relief, it did not occur to him to ask me why.

The cover of the last issue of OMEGA is now of a faded yellow colour and the pages inside look and feel distinctly fragile. The contents are made up of the usual pretentious pieces of student prose, shouting or sneering about the state of the world in general and of the arts and education in particular; the usual bits of 'challenging' photography and verse; the usual ingratiating advertisements from banks and bookshops and long-defunct restaurants. Some of the names of the writers I recognise – people who have since established reputations for themselves, though not necessarily for the kind of thing they can be seen doing here. Other names belong to people whom the editor himself would probably be hard put to remember.

And then there is this interview: one man talking to or sparring with another. As we know, and they did not, it was the older who was long to outlive the younger. Their words, smelling now of decaying paper, of ancient printer's ink, of the closed cupboard in which they have been kept, have in some sense outlived them both. They have even been transposed into another medium, in being set among my own words here, which smell at the moment of nothing but warmed-up plastic.

*

Diana claimed later – typically and perhaps untruthfully – that she had never read the interview itself; she could not be bothered with stuff like that. But we have already seen how she had tried to punish her lover for going behind her back to see her husband. She refused to meet Bester or to talk to him.

This was their first serious rupture. In effect it gave him a wonderful opportunity to set himself free of her. All he had to do was to keep away. By so doing he would transform the supposed punishment into a liberation.

Good.

It was summer. Better. His initial set of examinations was behind him. In Cambridge he had got to know a tall, pale, fine-skinned Canadian, Eleanor by name, a would-be cell-biologist by trade. Best.

Eleanor had a bony nose, a slender waist, and wispy translucent hairs that remained ungathered at the back of her neck whenever she piled and pinned the rest of it in a maize-coloured heap on top of her head. Across the ridge of her nose there were a few freckles so delicate in hue only her pallor seemed to make them visible. The skin of her lips was tissue-paper thin; it looked as if it would tear under the slightest pressure, and it had no more of a tint to it than her fingernails. Even in midsummer, even when she was out of breath, her cheeks were cold. When he kissed her she was dreamy and detached; she gave herself to his embrace and yet hardly seemed to notice it. She also had moments of cruel rage which seemed to take her aback even more than they did him. Once, when they were sitting and talking peacefully in a restaurant, she took the red, ruffled shade from the lamp on the table and simply thrust the end of it into his face, like a weapon; then she stared in horror at what she had done. Canadian fashion, she pronounced the word 'about', as if it were spelt 'a boat', and had no shame in doing so. Of the English-born students around them she said that they were 'either mice or louts'. Many of them still objected to a woman making a career in the natural sciences; such mice and louts they were.

She had no husband, no child, no more of a past to speak of than he did. She did not dye her hair. He was delighted by the slenderness of her bones and the inexpertness of her lips when she responded to his kisses. The surprisingly brief summer term was almost over. Each evening the sky seemed to retreat higher and higher, producing its own wholly unexpected tints of green; the brick and stone boxes of the colleges, beribboned and fretted with yet more brick, yet more stone, were forever being stared at by bands of tourists, to whom he and Eleanor were natives of the place, improbably enough . . . and all of it was just as it should have been, with nothing, or hardly anything, awry or shaming or anomalous about it.

Only – when he came back from a brief trip to the Continent he had made with Eleanor, he wanted Diana to know how well he had done since she had cast him off; and how quickly he had done it too. He wanted her to experience (if she was capable of doing so) something of the sort of jealous bewilderment he had had to go through, in the time they had been lovers.

But for her to know about it he had to see her, or at least speak to her. Obviously. When at last he did manage to get her on the telephone, and heard again her slightly hoarse, 'chinky' voice, he found he could not resist suggesting that they should meet again. She agreed at once. She had been missing him, she said, far more than she had expected.

*

By 'chinky', incidentally, he meant not that her voice was Chinese in tone, but that small, metallic notes came and went unpredictably within it. Hearing them reminded him of many other things he had by no means forgotten but which he had been unable to recall.

*

So their affair was resumed; but on different terms now. At first he thought they were to his disadvantage. The fiction that what they did together had nothing to do with what they did apart was abandoned. She had to be serious with him: that was how he put it. She had to tell him what she

77

felt about things, about everything; and she could not do that without telling him what she felt about her husband, now and in the past.

Which she tried to do. This was how they had met. (At a party, just after the war had started.) This was what they had done. (Gone that same night to his flat – from which, for fear of the bombing, his wife and child had been evacuated.) This was what followed. (He divided his weekend leaves between herself, in London, and his family in Warwickshire.) This was how she felt. (Inadequate, intimidated by his age and 'cleverness', fiercely jealous of his wife – whose pyjamas she had found herself wearing.) This was what happened next. (A pregnancy: which he dealt with by eventually divorcing his wife and marrying her, when Terence had been almost three; by that time Diana and the child, as if in direct imitation of his first wife and child, were also living in the country, to get away from the bombing.)

'And you? Did you love him?'

'Madly. I worshipped him. I still do.'

'You have a funny way of showing it.'

Diana sighed. They were in bed, lying together and apart. It was daylight. They were in his digs in Cambridge. He had long since moved out of his room in college; Foxborough was at a meeting of the European Broadcasting Union, far away on the island of Rhodes.

She lay in silence, on her back, looking up, her hands clasped behind her head.

'If he's so marvellous, why are you unfaithful to him?'

'That's because of me, not because of him.'

'Meaning?'

'It's my nature. I'm curious. Fond of you, you know that. Eager to please. I wish I wasn't, but I am.'

'Randy too,' he said, touching her.

She pushed his hand away.

'Hypocritical, then,' he said. She did not answer, so he went on deliberately, trying to goad her. 'Deceitful. Excited by deceit. It must be so, or you wouldn't do it.'

She turned her head to stare at him. He knew every thread

in the white of her eyes, every fleck of colour in the gleaming irises he was gazing into. She said, 'I suppose so. But it doesn't feel like that. It feels more as if I'd actually be a worse person, or a different person anyhow, more strange to myself, if I kept away from you – from us: whatever we are.'

'Well, that's ingenious,' he admitted. Then: 'Or is it just an elaborate way of saying you're getting your own back on him for being unfaithful to you?'

'Is he?'

'He says he is. He told me he was.'

'I don't have to believe everything he says to some little pipsqueak interviewer.'

This made her laugh; then he laughed too. Nevertheless his laughter enabled him to put in, as if it were a joke, 'For all I know you may have other lovers. I mean, right now.'

'I may.'

'Well, have you?'

She turned to him and took him in her arms. 'You're my lover today.'

*

It maddened him, nevertheless, that she remained so loyal to Foxborough. There was no other word for it. She would not tolerate any slighting remarks about him. She quoted from what Foxborough had said to her, and occasionally from his poetry too, as though both kinds of utterance had an authority over her which she would never question. She also said that what she most admired about him was that he was 'a man of his word'.

'Not necessarily his word to other people,' she explained, 'but to himself. He has an amazing capacity for making up his mind about his feelings – about what he wants to feel, or thinks he should feel – and sticking to it. I don't understand how he does it.'

'Sounds pretty cold-blooded to me.'

'Yes,' she said, as if she had not heard what he had said; or at least not the note of stiff resentment with which he had said it. 'It's one of the things about him that always amazes me. He really does determine what his emotions are going to be.

As well as what must follow from them. That's what it seems like, anyway. It's a great strength.'

They sat in silence. He used his spoon to grind some undissolved sugar crystals at the bottom of his cup. Of course what she had just told him about her husband was an insult to him, and must have been intended to be one: this juvenile lover of hers who knew that he wanted to stop loving her and to stop seeing her and could not bring himself to do either. She sat across the table from him, in a painfully well-lit coffee-bar off the King's Road, and amid all the noise, the glass and gloss of the place, he did not know which upset him more: the childishly obdurate affection with which she had just spoken about her husband, or the ineluctable signs of age he saw on the skin of the hand that was clasping her cup.

'How many other lovers have you had since you married him?'

'If I say none, you won't believe me. If I say three dozen you won't believe me.'

'Well, you could give me some plausible figure in between.'

'And then you'll stop asking me these questions?'

'No,' he admitted.

*

It was possible for Diana to say her husband's name without misgiving; he found that he could no longer do it. Neither his first name nor the second would come out of his mouth. Instead he had to use stupid and cunning circumlocutions like 'Your husband', 'Terence's father', 'he', 'him'; and, most resentfully of all, 'the poet'.

Jealousy of this kind was something he had not bargained for. He was the adulterous lover; let Foxborough be jealous of him! But it did not work out like that. It never had. He even began to read this jealousy far, far back into his acquaintance with Foxborough – or even before it. It had first sprung into existence, he now believed, when he had seen the man at dinner in college. The big-shot; the high-table guest; the distinguished poet; the Englishman – he did not know in which respect he had envied and resented him more.

80

And that was even before he had known him to be Diana's husband, too.

*

During this time he met the poet just once. It was by accident. He had gone into a pub near Broadcasting House which had a reputation as a drinking-place for people who worked in the BBC – George Orwell and Dylan Thomas, it was said, used to drink there; Louis MacNeice still did. My friend was with an acquaintance from the University of Cape Town who was visiting London, and to whom he was showing some of its sights; this pub, with the stories attached to it, would serve as one of them, too. It did occur to him as he went in that Foxborough might also be an habitué; and he paused at the door, as if to go elsewhere. Then he dismissed the thought. Foxborough worked in Bush House, a mile or two away; surely there was no chance of his being there.

But he was. It made my friend's heart beat uncomfortably to see him. Deep within the lunchtime throng, half-obscured by the bluish haze of cigarette smoke which hung motionless wherever it was not swirled about by the movements of the customers, Foxborough sat at a table with a group of friends. Those with him wore a kind of BBC outfit: well-worn corduroy or tweed, checked shirts, woven ties. Foxborough, by contrast, was dressed formally in a business suit, a white shirt, and what looked like a club or regimental tie. Otherwise his appearance was unchanged. His manner was the same too: detached and attentive; ready to be amused; seemingly confident that when he spoke he would be listened to.

'That's Rodney Foxborough, the poet,' my friend said to the visitor from Cape Town; and as he did so he remembered with a pang how the same seemingly harmless words had been said to him by someone else, in another place.

'Oh,' the other said blankly. His name was Elsmere; he too planned to become a lawyer. In the decades to come he was to win a reputation in South Africa as a defender in court of political prisoners. Now he was nothing more, in appearance, than a serious, bespectacled, elongated schoolboy, visiting London for the first time and determined to get the most out of it. Apparently the sight of Rodney Foxborough did not count for him as a major touristic *coup*.

Some minutes later he looked up curiously, as one does at the approach of a stranger. My friend, who had deliberately turned his stool sideways on to Foxborough, had not seen him get up and make his way to them. The greetings and introductions which followed were flustered on one side, calm on the other. Without being invited, Foxborough sat down at their little table. On it he put the mug of beer he was carrying. Beneath it he disposed of his folded-up raincoat. Barely moments later (or so it seemed), and speaking with a peculiarly intense mingling of relish and exasperation, he had launched himself into an account of a family crisis.

*

It transpired that Terence Foxborough and a companion, the son of a high-ranking army officer, were in disgrace at school. The two boys had stolen a tuba, of all improbable things, from the school music-room, with the intention of selling it to one of the music shops in the West End. They had not succeeded in getting far with their project. The manager of the first shop they entered smelled a rat; he questioned the boys, got out of them the name of their school, and promptly phoned the headmaster's office. At the headmaster's request the police were not informed. The two crestfallen boys then carried the tuba back to school, where they were interviewed by their housemaster and the head, who suspended them forthwith, and sent them home.

All this had taken place the previous day; now the boys and their parents were to appear together at the school – Foxborough looked at his watch – in an hour's time to hear the sentence that would be passed on the offenders. By way of explanation of his deed Terence had said merely, 'Oh, it seemed like a laugh at the time.'

'In the afternoon, when he was kicked out of school,' Foxborough commented, 'it no longer seemed so funny. By the time he went to bed it was beginning to seem comical again.'

'What do you think they're going to do to them?' Elsmere asked.

'Nothing too drastic, I hope. No harm was done in the end. But you can imagine how my wife and I felt . . .'

'Mm,' the two young men answered, with varying degrees of sincerity and discomfort. 'Mm.'

*

'Everyone's been guilty of committing his own particular idiocies, whatever they may be. Therefore you'd think we – I mean parents – would be patient with the follies of our children. But it doesn't work like that. Not at all. That's exactly why parents get so irritated when they see a child of theirs going through his particular version of the whole damn-fool performance yet again, on his own, as though no one has ever thought of it all before. What an utterly stupid way of arranging things it is! You'd think that if there were a Creator he would have had the sense to be a Lamarckian: so that not only could acquired physical characteristics be passed from one generation to the next, but acquired insights too. There would be some point to the wretchedness we go through, then. We could think to ourselves, "Well, nobody else will have to endure all this, now that I've done it, and seen the good of it, or the evil of it, or the hopelessness of it" – whatever "it" may be, you understand. Then everything we did, even our bad deeds, or especially our bad deeds, could be thought of as a kind of benefaction for the whole human race, since they'd be bound to yield a moral profit of some kind for the next generation. One can even imagine oneself deliberately committing bad deeds so that others would be spared the necessity of repeating them. What a luxury that would be! Then we could be self-sacrificial thieves; altruistic adulterers; kindly murderers . . .

'But of course whatever it was that created us – God or Nature, as Spinoza puts it – was quite incapable of a move like that,' Foxborough went on. He paused just long enough to drain the last inch of beer at the bottom of his tankard. 'It's too rational; too helpful. It promises us if not a happy ending, then at least a somewhat happier continuation of things – which is more than we're allowed to hope for now. Now we just have to flounder on until we're dead, and in the meantime we're given plenty of opportunity to see that nothing we've learned is going to be of the slightest use to those who follow us; that they're doomed to repeat all our stale errors and follies for ever and ever amen.'

He got up to go. 'Of course, my wife would argue that what I've just said is all very wicked. She believes in God, you see, and I don't. That's why she isn't free, as I am, to postulate a better working model of the deity. She simply has to put up dutifully with the one she imagines she's got. Did you know,' he asked my friend, turning his flat, elaborate gaze directly on him, 'that Diana believes in God?'

'No,' he said, 'she's never said anything about it to me,' and could at once have bitten his tongue at the intimacy with her which his answer implied.

Foxborough spoke imperturbably, with the same ironic good humour and irritation as before. 'No, she doesn't advertise the fact. She thinks people will laugh at her if they know. Terence knows, and he doesn't laugh at her. I know, and I laugh at her only occasionally.

'Now I must go and meet them both, and together we must face an irate headmaster. At eighteen I thought I would never have to do that again, as long as I lived.'

Then he was gone, leaving the two young men behind him.

'Gosh,' Elsmere said.

*

With a muttered word of excuse, my friend got up and rushed out of the pub. He turned into Langham Place. The wide pavement was crowded with people; the roadway with cars. Then he saw Foxborough's figure ahead of him. He was walking towards Oxford Circus at a brisk pace, his raincoat over his arm.

'Oh, Mr Foxborough,' his pursuer called out from a pace or two behind.

Foxborough turned.

'Yes?'

Coming up to him, the younger man wanted to grab him by the shoulders, to grip him fiercely, to meet his gaze from no more than a few inches away, and then to let him have it – all. *I know you much better than you think I do. I'm not nobody. You can't afford to patronise me. I'm important in your life;*

84

you can't guess how important. You must have some respect for me. I fuck your wife.

But he could say none of it. Cravenly, shamefully, he also wanted to say, *I'm sorry for what's happened. I've never meant to hurt you. I wanted to be your friend. It's your wife's fault as much as mine. More her fault than mine.*

So he stood there, scowling, staring, saying nothing.

'Yes?' Foxborough asked again.

Meeting the intense, indifferent gaze directed at him, he felt the conviction go through him, as if down to his ankles: *He knows, he knows.*

'I wanted to tell you – I mean – in the pub – I meant to say –'

'Well?'

'Just . . . there's a journal in the States, *Dalham Review* – they've written to Cronin about that interview you gave me. They want to use it. Has he already written to you about it?'

'No,' Foxborough said. Then, with what might have been a mocking emphasis on the last word, 'No one's said a word to me about that.'

'Well, they do.'

'Thank you for letting me know. Is there anything else?'

'No.'

'Are you quite sure?'

'Yes.'

They remained staring at one another for a moment longer. Then Foxborough was on his way once again, to keep his appointment with wife, son, and headmaster. His rival stood where he was and watched the assured, retreating figure. Soon it was lost to sight among the noisy vehicles and the multitude of strangers on the pavement: busy or loitering, solitary or engaged in eager conversation with their companions.

He returned to the waiting Elsmere. Their next touristic destination was the Soane Museum in Lincoln's Inn Fields. By the time they got there Elsmere had learned the central facts about the other's relationship with Diana.

'Gosh,' he said.

*

85

The only other person my friend had informed of his affair with Diana was Cronin. He had done it after the interview had been taped, but before it had appeared in the journal.

He spoke to both these acquaintances because he needed help and reassurance, and did not know where else to turn. But in each case he himself heard his confession being transformed, as it came out of his mouth, from an appeal into a kind of boasting. After all, his listeners had nothing comparable to speak of. The envy they felt was clearly visible on their faces. And if their expressions also showed their relief at *not* being in his position, then that merely made them look all the more like lucky but ignorant boys: fit to be looked down on rather than consulted.

TEN

Time went by: another laggard autumn, another hardworking but self-doubting spring, and then the same again, with the longer seasons of light and darkness between. To the surprise of both Diana and her lover (my lover-to-be), their affair continued. It developed a kind of regularity within its irregularity that enabled them to keep it secret; to keep it intermittent; to accommodate it to long abstentions from one another's company. Sometimes as much as two or three months would pass without their seeing each other, or with only a brief telephone call or two to keep them in touch. But when they did meet their intimacy seemed unimpaired. 'Like mother and grown-up son,' Diana said, only half-jokingly, knowing how much the remark would provoke him.

*

Quite a convenient arrangement, one might think, given what they were up to. Once again, or still, I really do not know how Diana felt about it, since I remain confined to my friend's accounts (all retrospective and prejudicial, of course) of what she did and said and how she looked. No doubt if she had had the chance to tell me her side of it, this part of the story, too, would look very different; almost unrecognisably so, perhaps. But she exists for me, she demands attention from me, only to the extent that he exists for me, and insists still on my attention.

Which he obviously does. For all the sense of failure that haunted him, I cannot deny him this great, posthumous success. Even before I began this task I knew that he had succeeded in infecting me with an obsession or illness closely resembling the one he himself had suffered from.

A long time ago – it seems a long time ago – I wrote of the

megalomaniac desire of writers to preserve their past; to save it from that all-engulfing vacancy into which all our experience goes; where even loss itself is lost.

OK. Now for a desire even more forlorn still. Picture to yourself people who are obsessed with *someone else's* past; who allow it, with all the ghostly, loquacious fullness they themselves are capable of giving it, to usurp their living present. That was his plight then, as we shall shortly see. It is also my plight now.

Admittedly, my obsession is not quite his. The context of it, the target of it, if that is not too bizarre a phrase to use, is different. But God knows there are moments, and more than moments, when his mania and mine appear to have become one. Still. Now. After so many years.

*

Let me be quite explicit about it. The longer the affair went on, the clearer it became to him that in fantasy, and in some form of mental activity that was even more insidious than fantasy, he had become committed to an insane, an impossible labour. He (or it, this fantasy, this self within him) wanted to do nothing less than to roll back Diana's past, to negate it, to undo it. Only then he would be able to share it.

And then – ?

He had no idea. In any case, there would be no 'and then'. It could not be done. No one could do such a thing. Even as a fantasy, the enterprise did not bear examination. It was crazy: no other word could be used for it. It frightened him to have discovered that he was even able to think of it.

But to take fright at the idea was not to expel it from his mind. By no means. If anything, the fear he felt seemed to encourage its growth. The dismay it roused in him helped it to creep darkly into every corner of his consciousness. So did his conviction that to harbour such an ambition was even crueller to himself than it was to Diana.

*

It showed itself to him, this ambition, in a variety of forms. For instance, as time went by he minded less and less that Diana should leave him after their meetings, go home, and (presumably) become Foxborough's dutiful wife once again and

Terence's affectionately irritated mother. He could even think with equanimity of her responding to Foxborough's caresses, a few hours or days after she had been in his arms, with the same involuntary repertoire of physical endearments he had come to know so well. That repertoire of hers was limited; it had to be so; she could not make up one *ad hoc* for every lover. He knew the pattings of the hand that were special to her, and where and why they came; the slakings of her breath at this moment or that; the sinkings of her eyelids and the unavailing fluttering that presently took place beneath them, as if something there was struggling to get out and just did not have the strength to do it. Also the filminess that always came on her lips, and its momentary, silvery elongation just before it was ruptured by a sigh.

Yes, he knew all these through her and knew her through them. Special though they were to her – and to him – they were 'ordinary' also. They were current. They belonged to the present. Let her now sleep with Foxborough, talk to Foxborough, go out with him, support him, give him whatever he demanded of her – by all means! None of it now seemed to him a cause for jealousy, as it had at first. Why should they not share her, after all, if she was willing to share herself with them?

But all those years past . . . That, perversely, grotesquely, was the thought he now found himself unable to tolerate. It was his imagining, or his incapacity to imagine, the years when she had not known him, but had known Foxborough, as well perhaps as other nameless lovers before and after his arrival, of whom she would not speak. It was the thought of what he *could not* in any sense share with her, and could never have shared with her, of all the time when he had been nothing to her, when she had been free to do what she liked and he simply did not exist – literally did not exist, because he had not yet been born; or did not exist for her because she did not know him, they had not met, and therefore she had no reason to take him into account: *that* was the absence, the infidelity, for which he could not forgive her, or himself.

*

He tried to hide from her as much as he could of this; but failed, inevitably. Once, with a mixture of amusement and despair in her voice which was familiar to him, she asked, 'So what do you want to be – as old as I am? You can't do it! Nor can I do it for you. And even if it could be done, do you suppose it would make you feel better? Damn it, I'm the one who should be full of self-pity, not you. Think of all the time that's still ahead of you and that's already gone for me. I can't look forward to any of it any more. It's past. I hate it for being past: much more than you ever can. It makes me feel so old already, and I dread growing older still. You speak as if all those years are some kind of possession I've stolen from you. They aren't. You never had them. I don't owe them to you. Anyway, I don't have them either. They're gone for ever. I can't take them out of my handbag and give them to you. Whatever they were, they're gone, gone, gone.'

'That's *just* what I can't bear,' he answered. 'When I think about this . . . gap between us, I feel as if I'm suffocating, I don't know why. It's the thought that I came so late to you and you came so early in my life that seems so wrong, so unfair: I can't get it out of my mind. It's as if I want to grab hold of – I don't know what – the actual machinery of the universe and turn it around, or make it do things that it isn't capable of doing. Justice is what I'm after! I want to be what I am now and yet also have met you years ago, you understand? I want you at my age to have been as full of me as I'm full of you, now, at this minute. I know it's all hopeless and useless – you don't have to tell me. It's like someone fretting his heart away because he can't fly, or because he can't pick up some immense boulder. In the end, what could be more contemptible? Or more trivial?'

She met this last remark unexpectedly. 'Sometimes you frighten me.'

'Sometimes I frighten myself,' he admitted.

On another occasion she teased him: 'Well, if you are mad enough to go in for impossibilities you could try and be a little more public-spirited about it. Why don't you have a shot at turning back history in general, for heaven's sake, instead of confining yourself to my little life? Why don't you try to arrange for Hitler to die at a nice early age, for example; or have his mother miscarry, which would be better yet. Think how many lives you'd save! What a benefactor to the whole human race you'd be!'

*

Painfully, with every month that passed, the lesson was renewed. His will could not command his thoughts and emotions; there were thoughts and emotions within him which had a life of their own, and to which the rest of him was subservient.

No, not subservient; not crushed and acquiescent; always resentful, disbelieving, angry, humiliated. Far from winning the battle in which it was engaged, this will of his seemed to be fighting a rearguard action against a hitherto unknown, incomprehensible self. All it demanded, this importunate creature inside him, was that he be admitted to the intimacies of a past from which time itself, space itself, the very nature of his being, excluded him.

*

And me? Doing much the same sort of thing, on his behalf? If I despise him for what he went through, then I have to despise myself. If I pity him, ditto. If I expunge all this, walk free from here, he vanishes.

*

Well then, let him finish it off. Break with her. Nothing could be more obvious.

The trouble was, he could not do it. Again and again he made up his mind that this time it was going to be done, or that he had already done it without even noticing. But sooner or later he would come trailing back to her. Several times he begged her to do the decent thing, so to speak: to exercise a strength he did not seem to have and to send him away. Let her refuse to have anything more to do with him: then he would find himself free of her.

Which she tried to do; or at any rate said she would do. But each time he came back to her and told her no, no, he could not live without seeing her; he needed what she alone could give him.

'What is that?' she asked.

'This particular torment,' he answered. 'The one I get only from loving you. *That's* what I can't live without.'

*

91

NURSERY RHYME

Inside his skull there squats a brain
(it's soft and white and quaky);
and through that brain there runs a vein
that makes his whole head achey.

For in that vein there floats a jell
(it's coloured pink, I think);
and from that jell a special cell
squirts out an evil ink.

For in that cell there squirms a worm
(it's ugly as our sins);
and in that worm you find the germ
where everything begins.

ELEVEN

Towards the end of his final year at Cambridge (summer had unerringly come round, yet again), Diana went into partnership in a secretarial agency with her friend Marcia. The first time he visited their temporary office she gave him a present of a batch of Xeroxes she had made. They were of her hands, her face viewed from the left and right, and a particularly blurry and incomprehensible one of her (clothed) bottom.

For a long time he treasured those Xeroxes; then, because he treasured them, he tore them up. No other woman he would ever meet, he was convinced, would be likely to think of giving him such a dotty present. His heart went astray in his breast at the thought of her twice lowering her lined face to the glass sheet and submitting it, for his sake, to the passage beneath it of that savagely glowing, green rod. And then again pressing her naked hands down on the glass; and then climbing on a chair so that she could clumsily lower her bottom on the machine, as she might have done in making love.

*

Initially the two women ran the business from one of the rooms in Marcia's flat. This was on the fourth floor of a red-brick Edwardian block which was just off Sloane Square. It had ornamental stripes of white across its front, like a rugby jersey. He went to the flat a few times in Marcia's absence, and he and Diana made love in the office, though never on the Xerox machine.

His glimpses of the rest of the flat had led him to conclude that the twice-divorced Marcia must be a small, fussy, scented, fluffy-haired creature: hence all the ruched satin to be seen around the place, the pink wainscotings, the pastel wallpapers and curtains. On meeting her, he discovered her to be six-foot tall and as broadshouldered as a man; she was dressed that day in a black trouser suit and a black slouch hat which sat menacingly on copious coils of dyed golden hair. She also had a wide mouth, a pointed chin and a forehead like a wall. When she sat with one trousered knee crossed over the other she revealed a mastodontic length of thigh, which he found inviting in some unwholesome fashion. He and she took an instant dislike to one another; and he felt a certain chagrin at the fact that (a) she was, according to Diana, her best friend; and (b) the business, for some reason, began to prosper almost from the day they distributed their first handbills to firms and households nearby. 'I don't know what you see in Marcia,' he said to Diana; to which she answered, directly enough, 'She says the same about you.'

'You mean, she knows about us?'

'Yes.'

'Who else have you told?' he asked, all the more indignantly for knowing that he had told his friend Elsmere (who did not matter, since he had long since returned to Cape Town), as well as Cronin, who remained in Cambridge.

'Nobody.'

For the tenth or hundredth time in different contexts he asked, not quite knowing what he wished to hear, and never knowing whether or not to believe her: 'Not even your husband?' and for the tenth or hundredth time she assured him no, certainly not her husband. Rodney knew nothing about it.

*

Strangely enough, in view of all that had gone before, an agreement that they should cease to see each other was arrived at, this time, quite suddenly and yet without drama or anger on either side. The effect was positively anti-climactic. They had given so much of themselves to the affair for so long; now it seemed quietly to become the casualty of nothing more impassioned than fatigue and circumstance. Diana was preoccupied with her new business; he was about to take his finals and then go back to South Africa for several months. When he came back he would move to London and be admitted to the Middle Temple and start the preparation for his bar examinations. Then he would enter his pupillage. His professional career would at last have begun. On his return to London he also planned (though of this he had said nothing to Diana) to submit himself to psycho-analysis. So alarmed and miserable had he been made by the affair; or rather, so alarming and miserable had he made it to himself.

Still, the initiative had to come from somewhere; someone had to prompt them to a decision. It was Diana who spoke up. She simply told him one day that she wanted to bring the affair to an end. All else aside, she said, perhaps he had finally succeeded in convincing her that the difference in age between them made the whole thing topsy-turvy, lopsided, sick, wrong, deplorable, etcetera. Still, she might have continued to put up with all that – as well as with the other guilts she had to bear – but . . .

Her voice trailed away. He did not prompt her. She went to the window and looked down at the traffic in Sloane Street, which never fell silent.

She didn't blame him, she went on, she didn't blame herself. But lately she had changed. Everything had changed.

He thought to himself: menopause!

All he said was, 'How?'

She realised that most of all she now wanted something she would never get from him.

'Which is?'

'Some kind of dignity in my life.'

*

That was what she said to him: this self-Xeroxer; this adultress; this pursuer of a man young enough to be her son. Why was it that her declarations could always move and surprise him so much? The sentiment was uttered so unreproachfully, he was filled with admiration for her. To her back, to her desperately dyed hair, to the little he could see of her profile, he said, 'If that's how you feel – '

'Yes.'

Then she turned and they looked steadily at each other. They made no move to touch one another.

When was the break to come?

Well, when he actually left for South Africa.

That was settled, then?

Yes. Settled.

He said, 'A long time ago your husband told me that you believed in God. What did he mean? Why have you never talked to me about it?'

She was not to be drawn. 'Oh,' she said, 'God? I reckon that if he's half of what he's cracked up to be, he'll forgive me for what I've done. And he'll eventually do the same for you, I hope.'

*

Which did not leave him any the less determined, on his return to London, to see what Dr Fainman might do for him.

It turned out that Dr Fainman had no trouble with our man, from a professional point of view. It was clear, the doctor explained, that he was driven by Oedipal desires of an unusual intensity. These were bound to have been derived from a fiercely repressed experience of what Freud had called the Primal Scene: that horrified glimpse, or more than a glimpse, he had had of his parents in the frenzy of sexual congress.

Hence his infatuation with a woman so much older than himself. Hence his prurient, injured obsession with the supposed richness of her sexual past and the poverty of his own. Somewhere, somehow, in that tin-roofed house in Bloemfontein, the wide-eyed, open-eared infant he had once been had witnessed and heard, perhaps many times, something from which his entire mental and emotional system had never been able to recover. The result? The allure of all women would lie only in the resemblance to his violated mother which he was compelled to seek in them and to impute to them. Equally crippling was his secret conviction that his own sexual performance could never be anything but a forlorn miming of what he had seen his omnipotent and frightening father accomplish. In some tormented corner of his soul he forever knew himself to be nothing but a timid mimic, a follower-on, a shadow of the real thing. Never in his own mind would he succeed in replacing or usurping the father who had preceded him to the place where he most wanted to be; for never would the woman beneath him actually be his mother.

That was not all. The fixity of his desire to reverse the order of time – something which he knew to be absurd and impossible of attainment – actually revealed the depth of his longing to return and remain for ever in the trance of alarm and attention which that scene, or those scenes, had aroused in him. To be helpless, speechless, afraid, a witness compelled, a presence that was also an eternal, claustral absence: in that condition he was safe; there nothing was asked of him but despair.

*

So far Dr Fainman; and very helpful, too, my friend found his account of things. It made sense, of a kind, of his own internal antics. It provided him with what he felt to be otherwise miserably lacking in the whole business: a motivation for passions which were not just irrational and inexplicable, but all the more magnetic for being so.

Later, while still admiring the ingenuity of the tale the doctor had told him, he was sadly to conclude that there was probably not much truth in it. As a description of what he was – yes, very likely. He recognised in himself the shadowy latecomer and self-negator the doctor had spoken of. But the rest of it could be verified only by Dr Fainman's own say-so; and that, his patient came to think, was not worth a great deal. He had no recollection whatever of the catastrophic episode on which the entire story depended. (Aha! says Dr Fainman.) Dr Fainman himself had had no *entrée* into the homestead of that railwayman and his spouse. He had never visited Bloemfontein in his life. He had probably never heard of the place until Adrian Bester turned up on his doorstep. He knew nothing of the domestic arrangements of that long-disbanded household. For all either of them knew, the infant in question may have been scrupulously kept out of his parents' bedroom from the very first day of his life. And even if he had happened to witness and overhear activities he should have been excluded from, who could say that his infantile perceptions of them had been not only so exact but also (or therefore) so permanently disabling?

97

Putting aside the primal importance of the Primal Scene turned out to be easier, however, than dislodging the optimistic assumptions which had brought him to Dr Fainman in the first place. These were: that to the shape taken by every passion there is an assignable cause; to every irrationality there is an explanation which can be couched in rational terms, or what is believed to be rational terms; to every ailment there is a cure.

*

Besides, even after having had him on the couch for one hour every three days in each week over a period of two years or more, Dr Fainman knew nothing of Diana's chinky voice or rough laugh; he did not know about her capacity to mime, in a flash, and for a flash only, other people present or remembered. Nor did he know about the peculiarly warm, dry texture of her hands; or about the emphatic regularity of her features (too much so for beauty) which was slowly giving way to something less emphatic and less regular; or about the pathos of the deepening lines across her throat, where it looked as if fine threads were being drawn more and more tightly around it, even as the skin became looser. And then there was that characteristic of hers which was more difficult than any other to describe or understand or come to terms with: her stubborn docility, her unassuming self-regard.

*

The two years while he was under the doctor's tutelage passed without he and Diana seeing, speaking or writing to each other. That was to be the longest period of abstention from one another's company they were ever to enjoy or suffer once they had become lovers.

For the time being, then, I propose to leave him there, on the doctor's couch. He is quite safe in that austerely elegant Hampstead room. When I want him to get up, to make himself available to me again, at whatever stage of his life I choose to revisit, he will do so unhesitatingly.

I am in charge now. Not him, not Dr Fainman, not Diana.

PART TWO

TWELVE

Cronin, the proud editor of OMEGA and friend of my friend, appeared for the first time at the beginning of this tale, more or less. He was one of the youngsters in the hall when Foxborough visited Nick's: the one with the fine skin, and the small golden moustache, and the fair hair, and the faintly trembling hands. A tall, thin man, he was.

And so he still is, though bowlegged now and also bent rather stiffly at the waist, as if with a slight, permanent, deferential bow. His hair, though reasonably thick for a man of his age, is quite colourless; and his skin, though still fine, is webbed with wrinkles; and his eyes have retreated under a pair of elaborate old man's eyebrows. (They start forward fiercely from his forehead and then trail away downwards like dejected or broken antennae.) As for the trembling of his hands – that is so severe it now has to be treated with drugs, and has made it impossible for him to drive a car, and shames him every time he has to produce a handful of change or lift up a cup of tea. The embarrassment of it was in fact largely responsible for his decision to take early retirement from his work, several years ago. Since when he has dwindled steadily in spirits and self-confidence.

But that, as they say, is another story.

Or is it? Is it indeed? This Cronin (not his real name, by the way) is the only character in the story so far, aside from its hero, whom I knew well, and know still. He was a presence in my consciousness long before the South African appeared. I knew him almost before I was aware of anyone else in the world. Without him, I would never have known anything of the story I have told so far; and the later years of my own life, therefore, would have been unimaginably different from what they have been.

*

So stay a little longer with Cronin, as he is today, or as he was barely an hour ago: a neatly dressed, elderly man, waiting for a bus after having spent a few hours with his half-sister.

The daughter of his father and a different mother, this sister of his is much younger than he is. Nevertheless she has always been much attached to him, and he to her. She has come to the bus-stop to see him off, despite his courteous insistence that there is no need, really no need whatever, for her to do so, and then to stand there with him; and especially on such a blowy, dusty day. To which she replies that she does not mind waiting at all; that there is nothing of importance waiting for her at home (which he well knows).

Then they both look down the dismal vista of the main road. No bus appears. Cars go by indifferently. Overhead darker and lighter clouds hurriedly assemble, confer, and separate, like delegates at a meeting at which nothing will ever be settled. From the pavement beggarly scraps of paper rise up every now and again, as if in acute discomfort, before dossing down again on the hard slabs, haphazardly, but especially in the bays of shopfronts. Two hours of daylight, at least, are still left to the autumn afternoon, but the sun has given up already, gone behind the pre-occupied clouds and vague but motionless buildings – evidently not to return. Across the road is a closed motor showroom, where stranded and distorted cars glower behind plate glass.

It has taken brother and sister a lifetime to get into this particular bus-shelter, on this particular Sunday afternoon. They share countless memories; each has more memories yet which the other knows nothing of. The last of the Mohicans! He asks her when Summer Time will come to an end and the clocks will be put forward; on being told they will go back, he says, 'I never can remember.' In the heart of them both there is a weight nothing can lift; but they never speak of it. They merely gaze at each other with an affection so tired neither is able to make any demands of the other.

'Probably four of them will turn up at once,' he says, referring

102

to the absent buses; and she answers, as if by rote, 'They're always like that.'

'Convoys,' he says with a wistful attempt at facetiousness; it is a joke she has heard many times before. 'They always travel in convoy – for safety – like ships during the war.'

'Yes.'

An onlooker or eavesdropper might well think of them as a married couple, they seem so much to belong to one another. The difference of years between them, once so important to them both, hardly seems to matter now. Her figure has thickened, her hair is greying, her face lined; though they may be a little newer than his, her clothes are worn less stylishly. Both of them are well wrapped up. No family resemblance is discernible in their faces: her complexion is sallow and her chin bulldoggy, as he used to say when she was a sensitive little girl, but would never say now, when she would not mind at all.

Well, she would still mind it a little. Some things are never given up entirely.

Then the bus appears at last – one followed by another, sure enough, as he points out with a smile and a lifted, trembling finger. His hand, quavering uncontrollably now that a demand is being made of it, finds its way into the pocket of his fawn raincoat. After a struggle, an agitation muffled by cloth, as if a small, suddenly awakened animal lives there, he pulls out his bus-pass. The bus stops, its doors hiss open, he mounts the steps cautiously; to help him to get up safely his trembling hand reaches for the pole in the middle of the entrance.

There: he has done it. Safe inside, he turns as the doors snap closed and gives her a shaky wave, which she returns. The bus pulls away. She stands at the stop for a moment longer, watching it go, unable to pick out his figure within the dark confusion of the vehicle's interior.

It is a relief that the bus has come and gone, and that their awkward vigil in the street has ended. Another of his regular Sunday visits is over. Their next conversation will be on the telephone two days hence. It always is.

*

103

Pretty trivial stuff, no doubt. Just the ordinary, inconsequential stuff which fills so much of our lives and so discreetly helps to break the heart.

Especially as I happen to know that she, his devoted sister, has been less than truthful in telling him that she has no special reason to hurry back to her home. In fact, she has been longing for him to be gone. She has a task awaiting her at home, which she has been compelled to put aside during his visit. He knows nothing about it. She had not even begun it when they had last seen each other, the previous weekend; and she has no intention, as yet, of telling him about it. In the meantime she begrudges every moment she spends away from it.

The fact is, she is writing something which is both autobiographical and about the life of someone else; which is autobiographical precisely because it is about someone else's life; which she resents, even hates, for that very reason and yet from which, after so long a silence, she cannot tear herself away.

*

There, so my secret, such as it is, is out. And so early too!

I will never make it professionally I fear, not in this wordy trade; not even if I sit in front of this highly professional machine for a hundred years. Imagine an anonymous narrator blurting out the secret of her identity just like that, half-way through, instead of hanging on to the secret for as long as possible – and then at some cunningly chosen, culminating moment, letting it at last be known. The final cannonade.

Followed by consternation and wonderment among all on-lookers, and a satisfied sigh of, 'Oh, I *thought* so all along!'

*

Nevertheless, I feel nothing but relief at having brought it out. Yes, I am Cronin's half-sister, and (so to speak) always have been. He is the older brother at whom I gazed with all the fervent admiration and wonder that younger children are capable of feeling for their older siblings.

And please, let no Dr Fainman (or equivalent) come prating banalities to me on the subject of sibling rivalry, etcetera. As if rivalry and a spirit of emulation have ever been separable from admiration; or as if little children, precisely because they are so conscious of their own puniness and vulnerability, are not capable of a love as close to selflessness, indeed to self-extinction, as any human love ever is.

For whom should such a love be felt, if not for their older siblings: wonderful creatures who are so adult-seeming and yet are not adults; who appear to be so free and who yet share with the child a dependency they can never entirely conceal?

That (as close as I can describe it) is what I used to feel for the man with whom I charitably and self-pityingly waited at the bus-stop a little while ago.

And as for his friends, the benign, deep-voiced, young men, strangers all, with their bristly chins and unfamiliar smells, whom he occasionally brought to the house – !

I did not love them all; far from it. But all were to be worshipped, in one way or another. A plumpish young South African no less than any of the others.

*

Imagine a black-brick terraced house in Islington with a flat, austere front concealing a strangely devious interior. Picture in it room after room, from basement to attic, stacked around a serpentine staircase. People those rooms with my brother (the child of my father's first, absconded wife); myself; a fluctuating population of tenants; and of course my ingeniously mismatched parents.

Turn now to my father – an embittered expert in pictorial books of the eighteenth century; an employee of the British Museum; a monologist on the subject of the fortune he would have made if only he had bought and sold the books he knew so much about, instead of merely studying and cataloguing them. A large, frowning, bespectacled, white-haired man (I have no memory of his hair being any other colour, or, for that matter, of its ever looking as though it had recently been combed), his feet were of a size I can remember being astonished by every time I gazed at them. His stride was correspondingly awkward. Clatter and scrape went his big black shoes, coming down the stairs; and damn and blast, and Oh Christ, Christ, Christ went his voice. Then he could come to a stop on the landing or in a doorway. His body always seemed to hang at an awkward

105

or unreliable angle over those feet of his; on his face there was usually an expression of injury. He wore dark suits with baggy, hoop-mouthed pockets, and half-moon spectacles low on his nose. The collars of his shirts had points that curled back on themselves. 'Donnish' (like 'eccentric') was a word he liked to use about himself; and I must admit that there were periods in my life when such wry, twinkling terms gave me comfort, too, when I thought about him.

Of his first, absentee wife I knew nothing: he never spoke directly of her, and no document referring to her, no picture of her, not so much as a random, overlooked snapshot of her, was ever to be seen in the house. In fact, I would scarcely have known of her existence had it not been for the incontestable presence – and absence – of that older half-brother of mine, who was mostly away in boarding school, and then in the army, and then at university, and then just away, out there, in the world. For the rest, it was only by way of a single, savage, frequently used phrase that my father ever acknowledged the fact that he had once had another wife. My mother, he said, was his '*second* great mistake'.

My mother's sole response to this insult was to open her eyes wider within their dusky den of mascara. She carried on a life of her own in that house (of which she and not my father was the owner), and felt that she could afford to ignore him. She was the landlady, the businesswoman: the one who found the tenants, settled terms with them, gossiped with them, and argued with them about the use they made of the bathrooms. Of her husband she used to say that he was 'very brainy' (this plainly being an insult in her mouth); and of herself that she was 'very stupid of course' (at which she would hold up her painted nails in order to glance admiringly at them, or turn up the points of her shiny shoes for the same purpose). Small and plump, with a full, firm bust and hair of a permanently jet-black hue, she was both untidy and incorrigibly fussy. When I try to recall her now, I sometimes find myself thinking of a starling. She was as black and shiny as that bird. And as grubby. And as unappealingly busy.

*

From an early age it was a mystery to me that my parents could ever have come close enough together to produce me, and that they should have stayed together, more or less, thereafter. Later, as an adolescent, I decided that they did after all have something in common. Each was ashamed of the other.

It was a powerful bond: no question. Even after they had formally separated, when I was about ten, they continued to inhabit the same house, as if each could not do without the irritation of the other's propinquity. They lived on different floors of the house, seldom speaking to one another but often exchanging hostile notes. My father took great pains in composing his communications to her; whenever he was especially proud of some sarcastic turn of phrase he had just invented he would read it aloud to me, before pushing the letter under my mother's door. He also used to take delight in pointing out to me the errors of grammar and spelling in her replies.

Somehow I grew up between them, in that narrow street, where our terrace of houses faced another exactly like itself (only in reverse, like a negative), with the same windows and doors and basement-areas behind railings; where the slant and colour of the sun, when it shone at all, and the cut of the shadows told you exactly what season it was; where children I was not supposed to play with played on the pavement, and tenants whose rooms I was not supposed to enter went up and down our stairway. (The sound of their radios and television sets constantly went up and down the stairway.)

How to summarise one's own childhood? Impossible, it seems. Yet when I look back on mine I discern at once some leading themes or emotions. Embarrassment over my parents, for example. Awe and gratitude towards my brother. A sense of having more space available to me than I could reasonably use, the narrowness of the house and street notwithstanding. Time, above all: time on my hands.

Schooldays or holidays, it made no difference. The brown and black winter lasted for ever; then it was succeeded by a never-ending, fluorescent summer; both were composed of individual days that seemed able, in some mysterious fashion, to extend themselves from within, and in both directions too, so

107

that whatever was over and done with seemed fully as distant, at every point, as anything – homework, supper, bedtime – that still lay ahead.

*

The result was that I was positively consumed with the desire for adulthood. I could not wait for my body to grow to its full size and shape, and to assume all its functions. Then the years of preparation in which I was entrapped would be over; then I would come at last into possession of my real life and my real self. I was convinced that all I was compelled to go through until then was just provisional, a period of waiting merely. Teachers and parents, as well as my own eager expectations, seemed constantly to declare it to be so. So did the intermittent presence in the house of my brother, so many years older than myself. Ahead of me I constantly saw a gleaming fulfilment-to-come, at once unimaginable and yet ineluctably mine, not to be denied.

And then at last I got there. So the calendar and the laws of the state declared; not to speak of my own body. No screens, no parents, no secrets, stood between me and whatever I could grasp of all that was offered to me. I was adult: I had become the person I was always meant to be.

Whereupon I discovered, rapidly in some respects, more slowly in others, that the real world I had been longing to inherit had somehow slipped behind me. It belonged there, in childhood, in that very state of expectation in which I had got used to living. That was where I had shaped reality to the only forms I could truly recognise, and where my circumstances had shaped me to a form coherent with them. There, in that world I had set so little store by, I had become the self I would always be. It was there that my habits of response and perception were formed, then that my affections and revulsions, and the limitations as well as the intensities of both, were irrevocably determined.

Now I could drink and smoke and have sex and stay up as late as I liked, I could drive cars and earn money and spend it. And do whatever else I wished. But almost all of it, or rather, all the ways in which I went about having these experiences, were those which my despised childhood had compelled upon me.

At least, that is how it seems to me. Here. Now. Going about this task.

And it is not even my life that is supposedly at issue here; but his, my friend's, my confidant's, my worst and most beloved enemy's. I mean, the man I blame for robbing me of the other, unimaginable lives I might otherwise have had. The one I cannot forgive for leaving me: leaving me still with so much time on my hands.

*

Of course, that is another subject for farce, as I have already noted. I accuse him of fixation, of pathology, of being a wholly appropriate subject for the ministrations of a Dr Fainman.

But then, for God's sake, what am I doing here, giving my life over to his yet again, recounting his story, obsessed with his obsessions, as little free from him as he was from Diana.

It is a farce: no question. How amusing I would find it, if only it were someone else who was trapped in it.

THIRTEEN

I still live in that house in Islington, by the way. It is worth a great deal of money now; more than I care to think about. It was my inheritance from my mother, who willed it directly to me. After her death, I came home. As the tenants left, the rooms fell back into my possession. The basement and the attic-floor are now let off as self-contained flats; the rest of the house, all three floors of it, is my own. For what are no doubt perverse reasons, I like it here. When I cannot sleep in one room I go to another, sometimes at three or four in the morning, dragging my pillow with me. Friends come to stay with me from time to time. To be the owner of a virtually empty house in London is a guarantee of a popularity of a kind. My nephew (half-nephew? – my half-brother's son, anyway) and his family were here from Australia last summer. They expect to be my heirs, in their turn, and the way things are going I expect they are right.

*

He must have come to the house several times, that man who was my brother's friend and was later to become mine, before I became fully conscious of him as an individual, the one called Adrian, a person I would be able to recognise elsewhere. I know, for instance, that he was staying at our house when, fatefully for him (and hence for me), he went to the lecture Foxborough gave in the City; but of that visit I remember nothing at all. Nor of others which he was subsequently to mention to me. Doubtless, in those early days, I responded to him as I did to all my brother's friends – with the same shyness and curiosity, the same disbelief that I would ever be as they were, together with an equally strong, contradictory longing that I might be so now, at once, and thus be truly admitted to their company:

110

not as an indulged and puzzling pet (a role I enjoyed playing, need I say?), but as an equal, able to take part in their late-night comings and goings, their eating at hours forbidden to me, the dangers I imagined their journeys and departures to involve.

Of the nature of those dangers I had of course only a child's fantastic ideas. They included darkness, getting lost, being far away from the protection of friendly adults, at the mercy of 'robbers', 'monsters', 'wars'.

As if all these are not truly to be found out there! As if we are not capable of being robbers and monsters to ourselves, too!

*

The time that has lapsed between the present and the distant past is like water. Distorting and half-translucent, weighty, all-enclosing, it seems to be another medium entirely from the one which we imagine ourselves to be living in now. As a child I used to go with my friends to the local indoor swimming pool, where we would throw a coin or key into the water and then take turns to dive for it. There it lay, this object, as if on the very floor of memory, its outline wavering in the dim light; above it passed my strangely ineffective hands, like ghost-hands groping for a ghost-object, at a distance from my body which it was always difficult to gauge. Then my right hand would touch it, fumble with it, scrape it along the concrete floor, grip it; and I would lunge upwards, proudly clutching something that had suddenly acquired a firm, sharp solidity and was now unmistakably mine.

That is itself a memory, the one I have just recaptured: seemingly non-existent before I began to write of it. Even the pressure of the water in my ears seems to come back to me now, and the sting of it in my eyes, along with the chlorine reek and all those yells and splashes between high walls and windows, transformed into a forlorn echo, a long-gone reverberation, reverberating yet again.

So it is with my first distinctive, unqualified memory of this man, my friend; the point at which he ceases to be confused with other acquaintances of my brother's, and becomes himself alone.

Well, not really alone, for I am there too, as I have to be.

111

And what do I find him doing in that strange space which my memory holds intact for him? He is playing a game with me on the floor. It is a board game of some kind, I cannot remember what. There is a lamp overhead, and, where the carpet ends, the irregularities of the varnished wood gleam with a bronzed light, above a darkness which is deeper inside it. I must be about – what? – five years old? a little more? – impossible for me to say. Later, without getting up from the floor, he begins to teach me a song in a foreign language. I can still sing it too, in an accent which never failed to amuse him. In translation (his translation) it went something like this:

Jan Pierewit, Jan Pierewit, Jan Pierewit stand still;
Jan Pierewit, Jan Pierewit, Jan Pierewit turn around.
Good morning my wife, here's a little kiss for you.
Good morning my husband, there is coffee in the can.

He offered me, I remember, a penny for every line I got right, and a sixpence (the coinage too has vanished since, let alone the person I remember) if I managed to sing the whole song through correctly.

How I wanted that money! – partly for its own sake, of course, but far more for the acknowledgement it would be of my achievement, and the praise I was sure would go with it.

In the end I succeeded, and was duly rewarded with both money and praise. By that time my brother had joined us. 'You're spoiling the kid,' he said, not unkindly, but with all the God-given authority of a much older brother. Then I was given another sixpence by him; this one was for 'clearing off, pronto'.

Which I did, proudly enough. The memory is a happy and untroubled one; or would be so, were it not troubled by all I know that was to happen subsequently.

*

A memory from what must have been a couple of years later brings with it a pang which is somehow bowel-like in its sharpness and intimacy, and yet is not entirely disagreeable. Anyone can feel something of that sort; anyone, that is, who commits a shameful act and then finds herself caught at it.

I had seen my brother and this Adrian come into the house

112

and disappear into my brother's room. What I had been doing before their arrival I cannot recall – chiefly waiting for time to pass, I daresay – but whatever it was, I put it aside to take up the position of eavesdropper outside the door.

Long experience of that position, not just at my brother's door but outside my parents' bedroom and the rooms of various lodgers, had told me that I would get no pleasure from what I was about to do. That was actually one of the perverse attractions of the activity. At best it was a furtive, sore-kneed, cold-bottomed business. I would not hear what I was trying to hear; both hearing and not-hearing, understanding and failing to understand, would remind me painfully of the wickedness of my being there; and of the sense of isolation and exclusion which had compelled me to commit the crime. In addition I also constantly had to keep my ear cocked for approach of any other adult in the house. If I did hear any such footfall there came a rapid, silent scuttle to some other vantage point, followed by a pretence, as deliberately childlike as I could make it, of being nothing but an innocent, preoccupied child.

Looking back, my heart goes out to myself, of course; never to those on whom I was spying. That I should have been so small! So ignorant! So pitiably cunning! And beyond that I am filled with an unavailing rage against time and the nature of our subjection to it. A moment ago I compared time to water; now it occurs to me that it is time which is immobile, unchanging, a kind of world-rock, and we ourselves the watery stuff which seeps through it, as best we can. Until we lose the struggle, petrify, and become an indistinguishable part of the rock, knowing nothing of the movement that still goes on and will go on for ever within it, elsewhere.

*

He caught me. The door opened and I fled, too late. The door closed, leaving him there, cramming behind itself all the light it had suddenly revealed.

'You!' he said.

He overtook me down the landing: two paces of mine, one pace of his. He touched me lightly on the shoulder, from behind.

113

'You've been listening,' said the voice of the man who was to become, many years later, my lover and my dearest friend; the one who took the heart out of me and left me here, remembering.

I had no strength to scuttle along further. He loomed over me, an adult figure, a face, a set of clothes, that seemed to fill the entire landing. My silence he took for assent; anyway he would not have believed me if I had denied it.

'So what have you heard?'

Still silence from me. Trembling and hot, I could only look down. Later – to me it seemed a long time later – I stole a glance at his face. His expression was puzzled and amused rather than angry; perhaps there was some pity in it too. I was on the edge of bursting into tears; suddenly I was certain that I could wipe him out, as it were, if I did so. But I did not want that to happen. For I also wanted, greatly wanted, not to spoil the occasion.

That must sound bizarre, I know. It is true, nevertheless. At last I knew what it felt like to be caught. A curiosity had been satisfied. A certain self-abasement had been achieved. Things had become interestingly, even if dangerously, unlike what they had been before. There was a trembling satisfaction in all this, a nauseous relief. Between me and the man who stood above me there now was an intimacy we had not shared before; one much greater than when we had lain on the floor and played that game and sung that song.

At which point, to my surprise, and quite against my will, I disintegrated into sobs and chokings. Hot tears seemed to leap out of my eyes and tumble down my cheeks.

He picked me up and carried me a little way further down the landing, before putting me down again.

'Don't be upset,' he said. 'It's nothing. I'm not cross with you. I won't tell anyone. I don't care what you heard. It was probably very boring anyway, boring grown-up stuff. Don't worry about it.'

I broke away from his grasp and ran into the lavatory at the end of the landing, and locked the door behind me. He must have waited outside the door for a minute before he said – and I heard with relief and anger the amusement in

114

his voice – 'That's where *I* was going. Is there another one upstairs?'

'No!' I lied, between my sobs.

'There must be,' he answered. I heard him move away. I was losing him. Time to unlock the door. But I had to do something dramatic now, or all would be lost. So, as I came charging out, I hit blindly at him.

I had no real wish to hurt him; it was merely my height relative to his that made the blow so damaging; not until much later did I realise, after a fashion, what I had done. All I knew then was that my flying hand struck through the cloth of his trousers against a lolling object, something so warm and loose it did not feel like a part of him at all.

The effect was dramatic enough. He gasped; he seemed to crumple over on himself. Terrified at the sight, I fled towards the stairs, on the way to the safety of the kitchen where I knew my mother to be. As I reached the stairs, I looked back. He was still gasping, still crouching, his contorted face turned indignantly towards me.

I did not see him again that day; or for many days, I think, after it.

*

So much for our romantic colloquy through the lavatory door and its immediate consequence. As for what had gone before, it is appropriate enough that so early a memory of our relationship should be of me, outside, listening for I knew not what, trying to understand what was going on beyond my ken; and then suffering the shame and pleasure of being discovered in the act. Only in this way would I be admitted to a world otherwise denied to me.

Still at it, you see, after all these years. Still cherishing the secrets vouchsafed to me.

It is almost as if there are two triangles in my mind which I have to try to get together as I sit here. They might be taken from one of those metal puzzles you buy for children in little plastic bags. It seems impossible either to draw them apart or to get them to interlock neatly; and yet you know that there must be a solution to the puzzle. The lines of the first triangle are made up by my friend on the one side, by Diana on another, and by Foxborough. The second triangle consists of my friend, myself, and Diana. (The memory of Diana, that is; the ghost of Diana.) They are separate and yet they overlap too, these triangles, in a variety of ways: morally, psychologically, temporally.

Of course when we were actually inside that overlap, he was the only one who knew of it; but it is inconceivable that he ever really saw it as one. What could his dealings with this child, with Cronin's little sister, have to do with his relations with Diana? No more than the child herself could he ever have imagined that, as the sole survivor of both triangles, she would one day busy herself by trying to reconstruct that secret relationship of theirs. What a crazy thought it would then have seemed to him, if he had been crazy enough to think of it.

*

And later? Much later?

Could he have known? Could he somehow have planned it – *this*, I mean, what I am doing now? Or even just have hoped for it?

The thought has never occurred to me before. Now that the questions have appeared here, on the screen in front of me, as if this machine has some malign will of its own, and has conjured them out of its own unimaginable circuits – now I can think of nothing else. It is like suddenly discovering that one is pregnant; and realising also, in the same moment, that the child one is carrying has been there for much longer than one's own stupidity has allowed one to acknowledge.

If this is so – *if*, I say again – then everything here is indeed his doing (with my connivance): his seed planted in my womb and left to grow there, to become our infant, the only one we will ever have.

Could he have meant it? Could he have been far more cunningly prescient than I have allowed myself to suspect until this moment? Did he foresee that one day I would be doing this work? Am I fulfilling his plan for me? For us?

*

He was always kind to me. I mean, he was kind in the ordinary, daily way of things. For that I am still grateful, all else aside. Since

116

so much of what I have to say about him has a reproachful ring to it, let me put that down.

Also, since he was prone to dwelling on his own weaknesses of will and character, let me say that he never appeared to others to be a weak or indecisive person. On the contrary. Even his build, his thick shoulders and neck, and his characteristic stance, with his legs planted wide and his head raised, suggested the force that was in him. So did his open expression. So did his manner.

He had many admirable qualities, and I am not going to let him deny me the right to say so. I earned that right the hard way. I suffered enough, and suffer still, from loving him. But then, there was much to love in him. Diana felt it too. He appealed to us for different reasons, no doubt; yet for all the differences between us, and for all the changes he had undergone between the time she knew him and the time I knew him – knew him as a lover, I mean – it was the same man who made that appeal to us. It must have been.

Hence my persistence at this task now. Or perhaps I should say: my obedience.

Let me not deceive myself. The suspicion I have just become aware of puts a very different complexion on what I am doing. It makes me think in a new way of the elaborate tales and self-reproaches I used to hear from him. It makes me view differently too all those pieces of writing he left behind: none of which he showed me; all of which I found among his papers only after his death.

Abandoned stories, fragmentary diaries, thinly disguised or undisguised autobiographical episodes, poems, unclassifiable paragraphs, the abortive 'Foxborough book', as I have called it in my mind – yes, I have used all of them freely whenever it has suited me to do so, and without acknowledgement. But I thought it was my idea to bring them together here, never his.

117

FOURTEEN

> *Can I avoid it?*
> No.
>
> *Can I go round it?*
> No.
>
> *Can I turn from it?*
> No.
>
> *Will I ever get over it?*
> No.
>
> *Is it the past?*
> Yes.
>
> *Is it the future?*
> Yes.

*

As far as I can make out, I must have been about seven when
I struck that painful blow at him. By then he had been involved
with Diana for some time. He had yet to arrive on Dr Fainman's
couch.

We met many years later by chance, as adults, as supposedly
free agents. There had been a few meetings in between, but
nothing of consequence. I remember, for instance, seeing him
at my brother's wedding in Hampstead Parish Church, and
our talking to one another at the reception afterwards, amid
the cream-pilastered and peppermint-corniced grandeurs of a
banqueting room in the Hyde Park Hotel. (My brother had

married 'up' socially and financially – and some joy and more heart-ache the match was to bring him in later years.) We stood at a tall window, this man and I, looking out at the trees with their swaying freightage of leaves, and the wide, peopled, weekend spaces of the park, and he congratulated me on how tall I was getting and how pretty I had become.

'You mean I wasn't pretty before,' I said saucily, fishing for a further compliment, confident of the status conferred on me by my bridesmaid's dress (a Liberty print), and my new white shoes and stockings, and by the unwonted sips of champagne inside me. To which he replied matter-of-factly, 'No, you weren't especially. It's happening to you now, though.'

A gratifying grown-up conversation, I felt this to be. And a further compliment of a kind had been wrung out of him, after all. For a few minutes I had forgotten my mother playing the *grande dame* at the reception; my father carrying on like the absent-minded don, remote from such prattling occasions.

*

That particular meeting I can date exactly, since I know not just the year of my brother's wedding but the day of the month too. It was a date that stuck fast in my memory, no doubt because I found the event so disturbing as well as exciting. (For one thing, I wished that I liked my future sister-in-law better. How could my brother be infatuated by someone I did not care for? Was it possible that his judgement and wisdom were not as profound as I had always taken them to be?) I was ten years old. My interlocutor must by then have been doing his pupillage in chambers; as well, of course, as confessing all to Dr Fainman.

A few other meetings of the same sort took place between us; inevitably so, seeing that he and my brother kept up their friendship through the vicissitudes of their careers: my brother going first into schoolmastering and then, through the intervention of his in-laws, into merchant banking (but never becoming the 'something in the arts' he had dreamed of being in his days as a student and hopeful editor of OMEGA); his friend and my friend-to-be . . .

Well, let him speak for himself, later. Let me here say only that we met just often enough, as I grew into adolescence and

119

then out of it, to recognise one another promptly when we at last came together on our own, out of context.

Incidentally (gentleman that he was) my brother had never said a word to me about our friend's involvement with Diana. I suppose he felt it to be beyond my comprehension when I was younger and none of my business when I was older.

*

I have said that we met 'on our own'. In fact we were surrounded by tens of thousands of people. By chance we were pushed together. A glance, a recoil, a laugh, and a pleased exchange of greetings inevitably followed.

This was in Trafalgar Square, at a rally of the Campaign for Nuclear Disarmament. I was there because I believed in campaigning for nuclear disarmament. He was there because he had promised his boss to attend the meeting and to report informally to him on it.

His boss, he told me over a cup of coffee some minutes later, was the Minister of State – i.e. the Number Two – at the Home Office.

'You mean you're a *spy*!' I exclaimed, aghast at what he had revealed, and yet at the same moment feeling my participation in the rally to have been utterly vindicated. 'You see!' I might have said to him, but did not. 'That's what we're up against!'

He smiled. 'Not really a spy, no. I'm not going to report on anyone in particular, I promise you. Not even on you. No, old — was curious. He asked me to come along and tell him what I thought about it all. "Atmosphere" is what he wants from me.'

'There must be two thousand policemen here. Can't they give him all the information he needs?'

'Yes, of course. But he wants something fancier. More subtle. More sensitive. That's because he thinks of himself as such a subtle and sensitive soul too. So . . . me.' He pointed with a thumb at his chest.

Though he had spoken rapidly enough, his voice sounded strained, careful, somehow rusty in timbre, as if it cost him more of a physical effort to bring out his words than it did for most other people. He was, after all, a foreigner by birth:

120

I had never fully realised this until that moment, until I had heard him claim to work in the Home Office, of all ill-chosen places. The thought occurred to me: he could be a spy not *for* the Home Office but *in* it. He could be working for someone else. The Americans? The Russians? The South Africans?

'I honestly don't know if I should believe you.'

His reply was no more than an ironic pursing of the lips and something between a nod and shake of his head.

For some reason this made me believe him. I too shook my head, at myself rather than at him, dismissing (with a little regret) the idea of his being a double-agent.

'So what kind of report are you going to carry back to him?'

'I'll tell him what he knows anyway: that the people here are mostly well-meaning, middle-class dupes, led by a smaller band of dupes, some of whom are well-meaning and some of whom are not.'

'Dupes? What do you mean, dupes? Whose dupes do you think we are?'

'Moscow's, ultimately.'

'You really believe that?'

'Yes, I do.'

'Just because I don't want to be irradiated and incinerated at the whim of some American president or general – that makes me Moscow's dupe?'

'Oh please!' he said. 'I don't want to be incinerated either. Nor do I want to lose the war we're already fighting; the one we've found ourselves in.' He hesitated, as if reluctant to go on; then took the plunge. 'People aren't supposed to say that kind of thing, I know; but the hell with it. We're finished if a real war breaks out, that's for sure. But to surrender, to chuck our weapons away because we're so afraid of a real, shooting war breaking out? That would be another way of finishing ourselves off. What you and your friends – the well-meaning ones – are doing is to make one of those things more likely to happen; the latter especially. Your ill-meaning friends know it, of course; that's why they're so keen on what you're doing. And that's why the Russians support them so eagerly.'

121

'Yeah-yeah. Them evil Commies coming to get us.'

'That's just childishness. I'm not interested in Commun*ists*, only in Commun*ism*. There is a difference. People are pretty much the same everywhere – obviously. The real issue is what their system permits them to do if they're in positions of power, or what it compels them to do if they're not. At bottom old — in the Home Office is the same human type as his counterpart in the Kremlin: I have no doubt of it. Neither of them would be sitting in his office if that weren't so. The same would probably be true of their counterparts in Nazi Germany – let alone the people at this demo compared with your average crowd in Red Square, say. The difference between them lies in the systems they live under, only there, nowhere else.'

'And what our system does in Vietnam isn't evil? Or in South Africa? Or in the Argentine?'

'Look, there might be a thousand things I loathe about our side – right here in England, never mind what goes on in other parts of the world. But there's nothing to love or admire or believe to be of any human value whatever in the kind of Communism that's in power in Russia and Eastern Europe. The entire apparatus is based on nothing but lies and fear: not partially, mind you, as any system is bound to be; but wholly, indivisibly. The result is exactly what you'd expect. If there were peace in Vietnam tomorrow, or if the South African blacks got the vote, or if the military had been kicked out of the Argentine last week, we, us, the West, Nato, etcetera, would actually be stronger than we are now. But if the people of Poland or Czechoslovakia could go the way they wanted to go, Communism would be finished. Dead. The Kremlin knows it, so do the people in Eastern Europe. That's why the Russians are trying so hard not to let them do it. And why the Kremlin values so much the help that you people here are giving them.'

*

Ancient arguments, I admit; now settled pretty much in his favour too, I must also admit; though he never lived to see it. At the time I was greatly taken aback to hear such sentiments from an old acquaintance, a friend of the family; a man who did not look or talk like the parodic, reactionary dope I would have wished him to be.

We left the coffee-room in the National Gallery to which we had retreated, and stood in the raised portico of the building, looking down on the shabby, vainglorious square below, and on the throngs of people now beginning to disperse from it. The speakers' platform had been built up in front of the plinth of Nelson's Column, between the attendant lions; it still bristled with loudspeakers and was bedraped with banners, but was now silent and deserted. It looked all the more dramatic, somehow, for having just been abandoned. A multitude of banners and posters, red and white, black and white, moved sluggishly above the demonstrators who held them; some fluttered, yawned, tilted, collapsed suddenly as they were lowered and furled. At every corner people were streaming away; with each pace they took they seemed visibly to transform themselves from a shifting, drifting, collective entity into so many disparate individuals, under the clouded sky. There was only one segment of blue above the dusky roof-line of buildings to the west: it was as if the world breathed through that blue space, so serene and empty it looked. On one side it was edged with a smouldering ruddiness; there the entire cloud would eventually ignite. Watching the crowd make off, I was filled with pride at having been one of their number. It was indistinguishable, this pride, from the conviction of being utterly ignorant of what was going to happen to me and caring not at all what that might turn out to be. The feeling was so intense I could only feel sorry for anyone who did not share it.

Him, for instance. This man, met by chance, who had been a figure of awe in my childhood, and whom I now saw to be nothing more than a plump, solitary person entering middle-age (to my eyes, at least), wearing his weekend sports jacket and open-necked shirt. Once again, glancing at him, with his grand-sounding and yet underhand reason for being there, I wondered if he was nothing more than an idle fantasist. It was easy enough to feel sorry for him, anyway: for being old, for

123

looking forlorn, for not being one of us, for cherishing such backward political views.

'I don't suppose there's any chance I'll find my friends again,' I said, looking at the people so full of movement; the buildings so hard and inert; the skies so indifferent.

'I'm sorry I took you from them.'

'No – no – it doesn't matter.'

Anyway, shortly afterwards I did find them. There they were, on the pavement below us: Andy among them – Andy who was and sometimes was not my boyfriend in those days. Looking at him in the throng I thought: he would stand out anywhere. Even his skin, let alone his tousled hair and pale brown eyes, seemed to me to shine with golden glints. Like the others, he was a fellow-student of mine at Edinburgh University. We had come down together for the demonstration; among them I was the foreigner, for they were all Scots.

I introduced them to my mature friend. I was longing to tell them what he was doing there – partly to discomfit him, partly in order to impress them – but restrained myself from doing so. Then off he went. When they asked me who he was, this chap I had sloped off with, I answered, 'Oh, nobody. An old friend of my brother's.'

*

Still, I wrote him a letter a few days later. I addressed it to him care of the Home Office, Whitehall, London SW1. If he had been telling me the truth, it would find him there; if he had not, he did not deserve to get my letter anyway.

The letter was an attempt to make up for what had later seemed to me my cowardly silence in the face of the attack he had made on me and my fellow-demonstrators. Also an attempt, of course, to make him take notice of me; to make him see what a serious and thoughtful young person I was. I wrote that I did not want him to think I was simply following the crowd in supporting unilateral disarmament. Nor was I foolishly optimistic, as he seemed to think, about human beings and how they behaved. Nor was it that talking about incineration and radiation gave me an illicit, unadmitted thrill, as it certainly did to some of the people at the demonstration,

124

both in the audience and on the platform. Nothing of the kind.

It was the thought of the last war, the one that had ended years before I had been born, that had made a unilateralist of me. And it was not even my feelings about the direct suffering it had caused – the devastation of Europe, the destruction of the Jews, the slaughters in Russia and China and Japan, the bombs falling around the house in which I had grown up – that had bewildered me as a child, and bewildered me still. It was, rather, the belief that all of it had been preventable. None of it, not the sufferings of one mutilated soldier or murdered civilian, had been inevitable. None of it needed to have happened. Hitler and Mussolini could have been stopped long before. The Japanese too. If different decisions had been taken at this stage and at that, in this place and in that; if different conclusions had been drawn from events and spoken words; if – ! if – ! if – !

That was what we had to struggle to remember: not merely that all the horrors had happened, which was hard enough; but that all of them had been unnecessary, which was even worse. They had all been useless. There had been no point to any of them. They had accomplished nothing. Now, whether or not there was to be a renewed catastrophe, I wanted at least to act, while I could, according to my conviction that it could be avoided.

To this outpouring I got a brief, unsigned reply. It was written in a neat hand, in black ink, on the back of a postcard. It said merely, 'I agree with almost everything you say. But in politics your motives and intentions, like everyone else's, count for nothing. Political actions have to be judged solely by the *effects* they are likely to have. There is no other criterion.'

I felt I had to respond to this. All I could do was to play him at his own game. I wrote on a postcard (which, for decency's sake, since he had given me no return address to write to, I put in an envelope and sent once more to the Home Office): 'Would you say the same about private life? Do motives and intentions count for nothing there?' Following his example, I did not sign this card.

125

In due course I received yet another unsigned card. 'In politics and public life you never know whose actions will affect you and whom you will affect by your actions. That is why you have to judge by results only, never by motives and intentions. Private life is different. We know each other there. In private life motives, intentions, and interpretations are virtually indistinguishable from one another. That's the bugger of it.'

*

So, over the next year or so, we became pen-pals. Irregular pen-pals, to be sure. Pen-pals who made no effort to see each other; not an uncommon trait among them, I suspect. When you sit alone in your room, nothing is easier to create in your mind than a perfectly sympathetic, understanding correspondent whom you can entrust with secrets you confide to no one else; someone who rejoices in your successes, grieves over your disappointments, and smiles at your jokes. Like the ideal reader of a novel, perhaps; or, even better, the companion you wish you could be to yourself, if only you were not given also to self-thwarting and self-hating.

But if you come to meet this paragon, disappointment is bound to follow. It turns out that your welfare has not been his prime concern, after all. He is actually much more preoccupied with himself than with you. It even becomes clear that as far as he is concerned you are supposed to be the supporter, not the one who is supported; the admirer, not the admired; the sympathiser, not the person who is sympathised with.

A fine anti-climax: no question. Instinctively, without even putting it to the test, I knew it would be so. Better, then, that we should remain as we were: I in Edinburgh, in the second year of my four-year Modern Languages course (Italian and French), involved with my glinting Andy; sharing a flat with three other girls; sometimes wishing myself Scottish and often congratulating myself for not being so; absorbed by the people and the diversions available to me in this grand, tilted, defunct capital city which I had provisionally made my home – while he remained a safe distance away in London, a friend of my beloved brother, a much older man, the holder of a mysterious and yet in some sense powerful job . . .

Perfect.

Perfect, that is, for a pen-pal; not someone of flesh and blood.

So even when I came down to London I did not get in touch with him. Though I urged him to pay a visit to Edinburgh, which he told me he had never seen, I did not expect him to do so and hoped he would not.

*

Now: a generalisation.

If we did not learn in infancy to distinguish one face, one presence, from all others, our chances of survival would be nil. Equally, if our parents, our mothers especially, had not been through the same process in their infancy, so that every mother attaches as much importance to the singularity of her child (in her eyes) as the child does to its mother's singularity (in its eyes) – then, again, we would be done for. The race itself would soon die out. 'What will survive of us is love,' wrote Philip Larkin. The truth is exactly the other way around. It is love that enables us to survive – not as individuals but as a species. Mother-and-infant love makes it possible in the first instance; and then all the forms of mutual search and seizure that follow from it for the rest of our lives.

Now: an illustration.

Andy and I are travelling by car across a sloping, soggy tract of ground in the Scottish highlands when we come across the following spectacle. Behind a wire fence is a large flock of ewes with their almost grown-up offspring. The wool on the back of each one is so thick it looks like a kind of quaking moss. Out of the grey mounds of this stuff, solemn black heads and paltry hooves stick out. On our side of the fence is a solitary stray, a youngster which has somehow found a gap in the wire and has got out, and now cannot get in again. Back and forth it runs, up and down the slope, bleating desperately; on the other side of the fence, in quite as great a frenzy, is its mother, also running up and down, also calling out incessantly. Every now and again both desist from their running to gaze at one another through the barrier between them, or simply to fling themselves violently at it. Then the running and crying begins again.

The rest of the flock goes on with its grazing, tail-wagging, chewing, dropping of pellets, lifting of heads to look at nothing in particular. Caressed by the wind, the grass flattens and straightens itself as if a living, catlike spine lies beneath it. Clouds move overhead towards small, mauve-coloured mountains on the horizon; the walls of a naked croft stand next to a pool and a couple of trees a long distance off. The ewe and lamb go on trying, as violently as before, to be united with one another, and fail, and fail.

Whereupon Andy gets his long legs out of the car. Golden hair bobbing, face ruddy, athletic hips and shoulders in constant motion, he tries to catch the lamb in his big hands by pinning it against the fence, or by stalking it quietly, or by running it down by sheer force and speed. Nothing works. It is too quick for him. Everything he does merely makes it more terrified than before. Now there are three crazed-looking creatures running about: Andy, who is not in the habit of easily giving up anything he has started, the lamb on this side of the fence, the mother-sheep on the other. 'Come and help!' Andy shouts, enraged by his failure. So I do my best, also to no avail. The lamb is too swift even for the pair of us. The nearest I get to it is a fleeting touch on its packed, moss-soft back; then it is out of reach once again. But I have seen the stark, brown-green light in its eye. 'Leave it!' I manage to pant out. 'Just leave it! We're making everything worse.'

Mother and child are still at it as we drive away. 'As if you can tell any one of those blasted creatures from all the others,' Andy exclaims hoarsely, out of breath, full of rage and scorn at them – and at himself too, for having failed in the task he had set himself. 'I hate animals. What I can't stand about them is that they're conscious, they've got minds, and yet they're so stupid. What's the old mother getting so excited about, for God's sake? Every one of those bloody lambs is just the same as every other.'

*

Another reminiscence, on the same subject essentially, but in a very different context. When I was a child in this house in Islington, I used sometimes to be overwhelmed by a kind of vertigo – half to be indulged in, half to be dreaded – at the sheer banality of the appearance of every member of the entire human race; myself of course included. (No, I did not know the word 'banality' then; but the concept was only too familiar to me.) All of them, all of us, had heads with eyes and ears, chins and noses in the right places; legs and feet ditto, with toes at the end of them; arms, hands, and shoulders where they were supposed to be; buttocks at the back, split down the middle. And if we did not, if we lacked any of these elements, or had them arranged in some way other than the conventional one, then the effect was no improvement; on the contrary, it was grotesque, freakish, incomparably worse.

That was all. It was enough. The thought of our sameness, and of the disaster it was for any one of us in not being the same, could come over me almost like a delirium. In these moods I would try to imagine what a creature from Mars would make of us: how contemptuous he would be of us for looking so much like each other; how hard he would find it to tell us apart; how he would despise us for sharing our shoulders and split buttocks, and the organs of generation and evacuation between, not just with each other, endlessly, but with dogs and horses and sheep as well.

Railway stations and airports were especially conducive to such thoughts, but they could come to me anywhere: in class-rooms, alone in my bed, even in dreams. So could the near-dizziness and the disbelief which went with them. I call it disbelief: actually it was a state on the far side of belief; one of entrapment, rather.

What were Andy and I to those poor sheep but Martians? Yet we had at least recognised their pain; they, idiots that they were, had not recognised our wish to help.

*

I have not wandered as far from the subject of pen-pals, or of one particular pen-pal, as you might think. Indeed, I have not wandered from the subject at all. This story is not really mine, not directly so; and it is certainly not Andy's. It is his – that man's, my former pen-pal's, my later lover's, and I am

129

trying as best I can to understand it; or at any rate to find analogies to it. Also to know better why I am compelled to write it.

A moment ago I said that airports and railway stations were particularly good places to feel stifled by our ever-changing, never-changing likeness to one another. By the same token, they are also the places which most vividly reveal the fanaticism with which we cling to the all but imperceptible differences between us. See the faces of the travellers as they emerge from the other side of the barrier that divides them from those waiting for them: how tense and hagridden they are, how they turn their heads from side to side, blind to all but the one set of features for which they are seeking. Then see the relief and joy which light up their faces, the tears that spring into their eyes, their craning forward as they break into a burdened run and their arms reach out to the arms reaching out to them.

For the moment everyone who greets and everyone who is greeted, whatever the relationship between them, is at once mother and infant, infant and mother. For each of them and all of them there is at that instant only one other mother and infant in the world.

No, I am not trying to sound like Dr Fainman. We would never have so great a passion for distinctions, for singularities, for this one person rather than any other in a whole world of persons, if we were not constantly besieged by sameness and indistinction; if we did not know they are eventually bound to vanquish us. For their other name is death.

*

After about eighteen months or so, during which time I must have received three or four brief letters from him, my pen-pal stopped writing. For some time I was vaguely aware that he owed me a letter; then, so far as I gave the matter any thought, I assumed he had got bored with our exchanges. This came as no great surprise, and I made no attempt to keep the correspondence going. In retrospect what seemed surprising was that we had started it, rather than that it had petered out.

130

Later, years later, when we met once more, I learned that it was Diana's death which had silenced him. Later still he told me about the manner of her death.

Over and over again he told me about the manner of her death.

PART THREE

PART THREE

FIFTEEN

The short gravelled drive had been built on a level slightly above the house and to the side of it. One arm of the drive ran straight towards a tottery, prefabricated garage; the other curved to the left and went around a circular lawn edged with brick, on which there stood a single cypress tree. Directly opposite it was a porch – an oblong box of glass and wood resting on a low brick wall – and the front door of the house. The porch contained an old couch, a pile of discoloured magazines, some shelves carrying potted plants, and, in one corner, a bowl for a long-departed dog. Through cracks in the black-and-white tiles of the floor there emerged grit, dust, and even some tiny threads of moss. It smelled, not unpleasantly, of mould and of dog (still), of the rain of many winters and the sunshine of many summers.

The smell of the house was quite different. There was woodsmoke in it, and furniture polish, and heavy carpeting, and the scorched paint of radiators. Beyond the hall lay a confusion of smallish rooms and narrow passages, staircases, landings, windows with wide views and windows that looked out on nothing but a bank of earth surmounted by a line of tortuous hawthorns. On the other side of the house a lawn, interspersed with rose-beds, sloped downwards to a tennis court and a line of trees; beyond was a vista of the irregular quadrangles and hedgerows of the tilled, populous Cornish countryside, stretching away to the sea (always out of sight). There was also a small, paved yard at the back, and then another and more neglected lawn, punctuated with daisies and plantains, decorated with a few rusting, tilted croquet hoops.

The house, called Sandarac, was the one in which Diana's parents had lived towards the end of their lives. It had then been bequeathed to her and her siblings: since which time they had rented it out on long lease and taken it back, put it on the market and decided not to sell it when a buyer finally appeared, lived in it at times of marital crisis, let it through a local agent as a holiday home and kept it as a holiday home for themselves. It was faced with smooth, pale brown stone, to which, on the sunnier surfaces, blotches of lichen adhered; beneath its first-floor windows were terraces ornamented with toy-battlement fronts; the many-angled roof was tiled with slate.

In that house, some twenty years ago, late in June, were to be found Rodney and Diana Foxborough; a couple of about the same age, Hadison by name, both of whom worked for the BBC; Foxborough's son, Tom, by his first marriage, and his German girlfriend, Birgit; Foxborough's very old mother, who was on her annual holiday from the home for the aged in which she usually lived (Dothecrones Hall, Foxborough called it); and a friend of Diana's called Annamaria Sarkis. Terence Foxborough had stayed with a friend for a few days, but the pair of them had left in something of a huff to go camping; they were expected back shortly. In the village nearby another of the house-guests, Diana's ex-South African ex-lover, who was there both as a friend of the family and as Foxborough's biographer, had also taken a room.

*

For that particular visitor the sole attraction of the village was that it was so near to Sandarac. It consisted of no more than a bald scatter of bungalows along both sides of the main road, with a small general shop at its centre, a corrugated-iron garage, and a pub hung about with dusty bunting. The pub had a tarmac parking space in front of it ('For Patrons Only'). Amateurish signs stuck on houses along the road advertised cut flowers, local potatoes and other vegetables, German shepherd pups, and Cornish clotted cream.

Our hero was staying in the clotted-cream house, which also did beds and breakfasts. He had a room overlooking a neat suburban garden, which ended incongruously in a wire fence with a wheatfield beyond. In his room he had put out the clothes he had brought with him, as well as a few books, a transistor radio, and some writing materials. If he wanted to watch the television in the house he had to join the Merriman family (Mr and Mrs and two school-age children) in their sitting-room. Mrs Merriman was a tall, stout, obliging woman; her gaze was sharp but she kept her curiosity about her guest carefully under control. Even after the catastrophe she managed to do this. Her husband was taller and stouter than she was; a shy man, he worked as the janitor in an office block in the nearest town. Their sitting-room was full of miniature items made of anodised metal (trumpets, cauldrons, candlesticks), varnished wooden carvings of dwarfs and fishermen, pictures of ships in full sail, and armchairs with fringed skirts down to their knobby feet.

My friend did not spend much time there, or in his bedroom. The only meal he ate with the Merrimans was breakfast ('Full English'); then he walked the few hundred yards to Sandarac. Occasionally he took his car. It was quite a comfortable arrangement for him, all things considered; more comfortable probably than he would have been if he had been staying in the house, along with the Hadisons and Birgit and Annamaria, and the very old lady, and their host and hostess.

*

The sea could not be seen from anywhere in the house or its grounds. In the evenings, however, there was visible on the westward horizon something which seemed to belong neither to the land nor the sky: a spacious, bronze-blue glow which did not change or waver, but somehow accommodated itself equally to cloud and to clear sky, and which stayed there until the sun had gone and the midges came, and darkness crept across the fields, over the hedges, up the last slope.

The mysterious presence of the sea, at once invisible and perceptible, was rather like that of the Cornish countryside itself. The view from the house was placid to the point of dullness; from the main road you saw little enough that was distinctive or interesting. Bungalow territory, it all seemed to be. But leave the highway and minutes later, even seconds later, you could find yourself walking or driving along hidden roadways that ran for miles between towering banks overgrown with grass and bushes, and that opened only on wooded streams, on sudden hills, on lost fields with tractor-scorings at the gates, like deep, much-corrected, never-finished pieces of writing, and burst-open plastic bags of fertiliser in ditches nearby, their contents spilt out and hardened, as if abandoned in a hasty retreat.

Eventually all the roads would drop down, alongside tortuous streams or wide rivers, until advertising signs and moored sailing-boats in the estuary told you what was ahead. There it was: just over the bridge, or just behind the high street, or on the other side of a sea-wall and a multitude of clapboard stalls and fish-cafés. Forever sliding and heaving its slate-coloured weights back and forth, the sea constantly whispered of effort and never showed any sign of fatigue.

That was one way of coming to it. The other was to cross some matted, rutted green field (let out as a car-park, often enough) which seemed to slope up towards the sky, so that the edge of land ahead became sharper, rising higher still against the haze, with each pace forward. Then just a few paces further and miles of cliff-faces would suddenly reveal themselves, as if with a single, giant shrug. The tops of the cliffs were all exposed rocks and ruddy earth, lurking shadows and sea-birds spinning and swooping like bits of charred paper in the wind; below, each cliff had a litter of froth and boulders at its foot, and, at low tide, a space of lentil-coloured sand stretching in front of it.

At once motionless and ashiver, the sea also appeared to be tilted upwards to the horizon; at its vanishing point it looked as though it was leaning against a sky almost always firmer than itself.

*

Some way down the coast there is one particular cove which is like all the others and unlike them also; for no two are exactly the same. On both sides of it sharp prows of rock jut into the sea, with broken ridges of boulders stretching out at the end of them. Revealed in all their confusion at low tide, largely hidden when the sea rises, at all times those boulders are a source of sounds of many kinds: thuds, hisses, sighs, whoopings, gobblings almost like laughter, immense cannonades which echo each other and send their bursts of shrapnel-spray flying into the air.

In the middle of the cove there is a beach of reddish sand where rubbish of all kinds – pebbles and bits of plastic, weeds and splintered planks – accumulates and is dispersed daily. Behind the beach more boulders still are piled against the base of the cliff-walls, which meet in the middle to form a ragged 'v'. One side of the 'v' seems to lean back; the other forward. Like a loaf from which someone has hacked a jagged slice, each of the walls is serrated and uneven as far up as you can see. At the very point where they meet, a sunless crack, so tall and narrow it is more like a crevasse than a cave, cuts inland from the beach for some yards and then peters out into so much fallen rock and lingering, murky water.

From a distance the walls of the cove are grey and reddish, with darker patches. When the sun sinks in the afternoon these patches grow darker still, while dints of bronze and silver come to life everywhere on the rock. Only when you are down on the beach, looking up, can you see that the cliff-sides are also scurfed with white, tufted at random with obstinate bits of growth, veined and wrinkled everywhere. To gaze upwards is like seeing a wild animal at close quarters and realising how scarred and battered it is, how much random life lives off its life. Then your eye is caught by a kind of path coming up from the rocks and ascending the cliff-face for some thirty feet, before reaching a flat ledge hardly wider than the path itself, which ends at that point. Immediately above it the cliff rises sheer again – uneven, cracked, impossible to ascend.

*

If this cove has a name, I never learned it; it was never given to me. My curiosity about it once took me to the reference section of the local public library, where I asked for the Ordnance Survey map of that particular section of the south Cornish coast. I had somehow imagined beforehand that when I looked at the map I would know instinctively which of the multitude of lacy indentations represented there was the one that mattered.

(Of this expedition I said nothing at all to my informant, then or later.)

But I was disappointed in my search. Nothing happened. My finger was not irresistibly drawn to one particular spot rather than to any of the others. So I folded up the map and returned it to the young man behind the desk.

SIXTEEN

In that cove – just as I have described it; or just as it was described to me – Diana met her death.

The verdict at the inquest was 'death by misadventure (drowning)'. According to the report in the *Western Morning News* evidence was given by Mr Adrian Bester, a civil servant (Home Office) who had been with the deceased at the time of her death; by her husband; by Mrs Annamaria Sarkis; by Mrs Clara Hadison; and by the police, who had found the body on some rocks several miles down the coast. The coroner expressed his sympathy with the bereaved and spoke of the sense of loss which Mrs Foxborough's death had caused not just within her family but also in her large circle of friends. He also advised all holiday-makers in the area to draw a general lesson from 'this unfortunate event'. In taking advantage of the beauties and amenities of the coastline ('of which we are so proud') it 'behoved them' always to be alert to its dangers.

No word was said at the inquest to suggest that Diana's death had been anything but an accident. Neither then nor later was my friend ever to challenge Foxborough with his accusations. He was convinced that to others his suspicions would have seemed at best unprovable and at worst demented. (Who would believe such stories about a well-known poet and a high-up official in the BBC? . . .) And even if proof of some inconceivable kind had fallen into his hands, what would he have done with it? What good would it have been to him? Or to Diana? Would it have brought her back?

Poor thing, she would not even have wished to come back on such terms – knowing what he knew about her husband and what had been done to her.

So he saved it all: saved it for me: saved it (as I now believe) for just such an occasion as this.

*

A picnic meal on the cliffs (potted crab and sliced meat bought in town, bread rolls, uncut tomatoes, fruit, white wine, paper cups and plates); tea with scones and clotted cream on the lawn; mornings spent swimming and sunbathing in one or another of the seaside coves; a few energetic but unconvincing games of tennis; newspapers and books read on the terrace; a visit to the village pub; a walk along the bank of a river, with much consulting on the way of the Ordnance Survey map; a drive to a shabby Elizabethan manor house, amateurishly open to visitors – these were the activities, spread out over different days and among different groups, with which the holiday-makers passed the time. Every day volunteers had to be found to stay behind to do the 'granny-sitting' for old Mrs Foxborough, who could not be left on her own and was too enfeebled to go on any of the excursions organised by the others. The granny-sitters were also given the duty of preparing a simple dinner (a stew or a plate of pasta, a thick soup or a roast) to be eaten in the evening.

Everything, then, appeared to be just as it should have been for a successful country holiday. Even the weather was kind. It rained often, but almost always at night, so that they woke each morning to shining lawns, to water-weighted flowers, to myriads of leaves beaded with single drops, to washed skies and white clouds heaped up harmlessly in the distance.

*

Long afterwards at least one member of the group was some-times tempted to see those days as having been charged with a perfection, even an innocence, he was never to know again, and which (like so much else!) he had failed to value when it was offered to him. In other moods he would insist that the holiday together had never been anything but a mistake, a bad idea, an enthusiasm of Diana's which she herself knew to have been misguided from the day the party assembled. Ill-feeling and bad temper abounded among the guests; so did passions more difficult to express and to give a name to.

142

The rock music which blared out from the open windows of the younger people's bedrooms was one continuing source of friction. There were others. People argued over what they should do next and who should be involved in the doing of it. There were disagreements about politics, about what to watch on the television, and about the use of the cars available to them. Some members of the party were silent and seemed oppressed by the company; Tom's girl Birgit, on the other hand, whose English was halting but insistent, talked far too much. Whereupon Terence and his friend got their revenge against her in the traditional fashion of the English young when confronted with anything German: behind her back they goose-stepped, gave Hitler salutes, and muttered, 'Ve haff vays of making you shuddup.'

In any case, Terence had always got on badly with his half-brother; the presence in the house and in Tom's bedroom of the provocatively be-shorted and be-shirted Birgit, with her long legs and waist, and her gaze fixed expressionlessly just a few inches in front of her face, did not improve matters. So off Terence and his friend went, in one of the cars, to the relief of everyone else. Old Mrs Foxborough was often in pain, sometimes confused, always demanding. She was especially puzzled by Adrian Bester's presence: first of all because he did not sleep in the house yet was always there; secondly because she appeared to be convinced that he was there not as a friend of Diana or her husband but of one of her young grandsons. This mistake was so irritating and so embarrassing to him he sometimes suspected her of getting a malicious pleasure out of choosing to make it. Was she also putting on a performance: this quavering-voiced, incongruously powdered, lipsticked, floral-frocked old lady for whom a bedroom had been made up downstairs and who tottered out of it for meals or to sit on the terrace in the sun?

He did not know. It was possible. Anything was possible among them. Look at Annamaria. Look at Foxborough. Look at Diana. Look at him.

Diana with the mature and violent caresses she had once lavished on him, and the childlike charm she still intermittently

exercised over him; Foxborough with his apparently aloof toler-
ance (indistinguishable from disdain), his cryptic humour, his
intense unseeing gaze – together they had been the undoing
of him.

He had been enslaved. Or paralysed. He had become the
eunuch in their little court.

*

On the terrace, then, at evening, facing westwards, looking
into an elaborate arra_ of clouds and fractured sunlight, sit
Diana, Annamaria, Mrs Foxborough, and my friend. Diana
has just under one day to live. The Hadisons are away on
an expedition of their own. Foxborough is inside the house,
working.

On one side is a table with abandoned tea-things; on the lawn
next to it lie a pair of badminton rackets and a shuttlecock.
Annamaria and Diana sit together on a wooden bench; bare,
female arms and heads of contrasting colour – one black, one
lacquered yellow – side by side. They make up one couple.
Another consists of my friend and Mrs Foxborough who are
sitting on a cushioned couch with an awning above it. In the
drive, just visible if you turn your head to look in that direction,
Tom Foxborough is fiddling with an ungainly motor-boat, on
a wheeled trailer, which he and Birgit have dragged out of
the garage. The name of the boat (it is also called *Sandarac*)
is painted in square blue letters on its prow; it belongs to
Diana's brother-in-law, her sister's husband, who has given
them permission to use it. Tom is fiddling with the motor;
Birgit, like a child pretending to be an adult, sits at the helm,
several feet above ground, turning the motor on and off, or
pressing the accelerator and releasing it, as Tom's shouts and
hand-signals dictate. The noise is worse than the music they
usually play, according to Diana; to which Annamaria answers
optimistically: 'Well, at least we'll get something out of it when
he's finished – and that's more than you can say about the
music.'

Between two bursts of noise Mrs Foxborough says to her
companion on the couch, 'Shouldn't you be helping Tom?'

'I'm no good at that sort of thing.'

144

'Does Tom know what he's doing?'

'It looks as though he does. Sounds like it too.'

'Edwin,' Mrs Foxborough says, invoking with an unmistakable waspishness the name of Diana's brother-in-law, 'would be most upset if Tom did anything wrong.'

'I'm sure he won't.'

Even this desultory conversation becomes impossible for a while, because of a particularly loud and prolonged outburst from the motor. No sooner does it stop than an altercation breaks out between Tom and Birgit. Birgit's voice rises to a single, sustained note of resentment and denial; then, like a child banished from a playground, she scrambles out of the boat and clambers down via the struts of the trailer. Her departure from the scene – big head, copious curls, stiff back, injured gait, sandals gaping and closing at bare heels – is silent but undignified.

'Well – ' says Annamaria.

'Your chance to help Tom,' says Diana to my friend.

'Thanks,' he answers sarcastically, but gets to his feet, all the same.

He is forestalled by Tom, who also abandons the boat and comes loping over to them. He is a tall, slender, shiny-faced young man, with something of his father's cast of countenance, though in a more scowling and contracted form, especially about the bridge of his nose and in the set of his lips. A prematurely deep line is scored across his forehead, intensity of feeling or self-preoccupation having put it there. He wears small, round-rimmed spectacles with earpieces that burrow into the exposed, tender flesh above his ears. His long hair is tied back in a pony-tail; his shirt is open at a hairy chest; his legs are displayed to full advantage in denim shorts and a pair of sandals. His face and forearms have oil-smears on them. Without acknowledging the presence of the others, he crosses to the table on which the tea-things stand, picks up the teapot in both large hands, and feels its temperature. Then he returns it to the table with an expression of disgust.

'Shit!'

'You can always boil another kettle,' calls out his father, who has come unobserved through the door of the living-room on to the terrace.

*

Tom does not answer. He contents himself with taking a plate with two buttered scones still on it. Head down, sitting on a cast-iron garden chair which has lozenge and flower-shapes cut out of it, as if by a biscuit-cutter, he begins to eat the scones with great concentration and rapidity.

Foxborough joins the pair on the couch. My friend gets up, goes off a few paces, and sprawls full-length on the lawn.

'How's the work?' asks Diana; to which her husband makes a weary gesture, signifying that he does not want to talk about it. His expression suggests that he does not want to talk to her about anything. Just a few moments later, all the same, he is holding forth to them in a fashion quite as intent as his son's had been in devouring the scones. By now, the scones disposed of, Tom is sitting with his hands clasped behind his head, under his pony-tail. Head thrown back, eyes closed, he makes no pretence at listening to his father. Mrs Foxborough too is inattentive, scribbling patterns with one finger on the floral material which covers her thigh. The other three are dutiful enough, however; or seem to be so.

Apparently Foxborough has not actually been working. ('And not working when you should be working is usually much the more tiring of the two activities.') What had led him astray was a book about Cornish history he had found in the bookshelf. Reading it has reminded him for various reasons of the time he had once spent in Finland – another fretted, broken headland (of a kind) sticking out into another sea; one so much bigger than Cornwall, however; big enough for the language of the people who lived there to have survived centuries of conquest and colonisation by the Swedes, as the language of the Cornish had *not* been able to survive occupation by the Saxons and English.

Which leads him on to the Germanic distinction between 'historic' and 'non-historic' peoples – the latter composed of all those small, obdurate, unimportant groups (Czechs, Serbs,

Croats, Finns probably, Cornish certainly) who lived or died in the interstices left to them by the historic peoples. Were the Poles an historic or a non-historic people? (They had had an empire once, a long, long time ago.) And the Irish? And the Boers – ?

'The Boers are absolutely obsessed by their own history,' his guest puts in. 'So are the Poles and the Irish. How can you possibly call them "non-historical"?'

'Easily. Rightly. Non-historic peoples are always obsessed by the miseries of their past. They have nothing else to boast about. But the rest of us can afford to take a more *welthistorische* view of things.'

He turns to Tom. 'You should ask Birgit what that means. All Germans know what it means, even ones like Birgit.'

Tom lets this pass without so much as opening his eyes.

'That's a neat trick,' says my friend. 'Borrowing a German word in order to patronise the Germans, as well as everyone else.'

'World-historical.' This explanation comes suddenly from Annamaria. 'That word Rodney just said. It means world-historical, right?'

'Right,' Foxborough assures her.

'Anyway, it's an old English custom, to patronise other people,' Annamaria goes on. Her speech is slightly stiff, but fluent. 'I meet it all the time. It doesn't bother me.'

'I can't believe anyone would have the impudence to try to patronise you,' Foxborough says, looking directly at her.

In the silence that follows they become aware, one after another, that Mrs Foxborough has fallen asleep. Her chin has sunk down towards her chest, to the flat place where her bosom once was. Her fingers are idle in her lap.

*

Foxborough sighs; Annamaria and Diana exchange looks both fatigued and compassionate; Tom gazes curiously at his grandmother. In the west a world-historical sky composes itself out of molten-edged clouds and fierce bronze rays probing upwards at nothing in particular. Behind the rays, above them, are immeasureable, gleaming distances. A few inches from my

147

friend's hand the plastic shuttlecock from the badminton set lies on the mown turf. It looks like the full headdress of a minuscule Red Indian chief. The fields beyond the hedge are furred with light.

A smell of frying onions suddenly comes to them on the still air. Birgit's doing, no doubt, in starting the preparation of the evening meal.

My friend says, 'Anyway, when I spoke of the Boers a moment ago I should have said "we", not "they".'

'If you really wished to think of the Boers as "we" and not "they",' Foxborough answers, 'you would never have left South Africa. You wouldn't be an English civil servant today.'

Getting to his feet the self-proclaimed Boer says, 'Sure, you're right. It's farcical really. I left South Africa because I wanted to be free. Unbounded. I really believed that I could do it. Over there everyone and everything around me was telling me what I should be. There was a whole bloody history that insisted on filling me in, slotting me in, and I was determined not to let it do so. I wasn't going to be trapped by any of it. I was going to be the one to determine the possibilities open to me; me alone; nobody else.'

Initially he had seemed to be speaking to Foxborough; by now his gaze is fixed on Diana. She drops her head in apparent confusion. Tom looks from the one to the other of them with a lowering of his head and a scowl-like deepening of the line across his brow.

My friend turns away and says to nobody in particular, and as if amused, 'And look what I've done! Look at the result!'

He has not spoken loudly. Nevertheless something about his tone wakens Mrs Foxborough with a shudder. 'What?' she asks, looking around in bewilderment, unable to focus on anything. 'What?'

'It's all right,' Diana says. 'There's nothing to worry about.'

Mrs Foxborough clutches at her son's hand, which is lying next to hers on the couch. Silently he disengages his fingers from her grasp.

With a theatrical gesture which seems to take in the view and the evening light, and which contrasts oddly with her didactic

148

manner of speech, Annamaria says, 'No one ever gets what they expect. Why do you sound so sorry for yourself? You should avoid self-pity. Self-pity is not manly.'

Diana rises abruptly. 'I must go and help inside.'

But Foxborough is reluctant to let go. 'That's exactly my point. You can take everything away from the non-historical peoples except their self-pity. The more you take from them the sorrier for themselves they feel.'

Diana has busily and noisily set about collecting the tea-things. 'Time for drinks,' she says, to which her husband responds, 'I'll say!' The group breaks up. Only old Mrs Foxborough remains where she is, uneasy, immobilised, disregarded. Foxborough and Tom wander off towards the motor-boat, my friend goes back to his room in the Merrimans' house where, to the best of his ability, he begins to reconstruct on paper as much as he can of the conversation in which he has just been engaged.

SEVENTEEN

For some time now he had been writing down Foxborough's remarks; he had also been reconstructing (in bits and pieces) what he could remember of their earlier exchanges. Ostensibly his purpose in doing this was to collect material for the biographical and critical study of the poet which he hoped one day to publish. Foxborough had not merely approved of the project; he was the one who had suggested it. 'Why don't you have a go?' he had said. 'If it's got to be done – and I suppose it will be done in some fashion, sooner or later – you know as much about me as anyone else is ever likely to.'

So 'the Foxborough book' had come into being. But whatever the writer's original, Boswell-like intentions with it may have been, it had soon become almost as disordered as most of the other pieces of writing he left behind. His record of conversations with Foxborough was jumbled together with accounts of conversations he had had with Diana, some recent, some that had taken place years before, as well as recollections of moments they had shared and descriptions of places they had been to. In this book, as in the others, there were also many entries consisting of just a few sentences strung together, or single sentences, or even lists of words of apparently special meaning to him, as well as rough doodlings, and expletives in shaded, 'three-dimensional' block letters.

*

Since I heard so much from him about the subjects that haunted him, placing all but the very briefest of these scribblings in context has not been difficult for me. The only ones I have not bothered with are those written in Afrikaans. There are so few of them and they are so brief I have not bothered to consult anyone who could help me with them.

Which reminds me. The Afrikaans language, his native tongue, was a kind of private resource for him; he returned to it every now and again, unpredictably, especially as he grew older. It was the language he often chose to swear in; he sometimes used to speak to himself in it. Increasingly, towards the end, his nocturnal cries and mutterings revealed it to be also the language in which he dreamed.

*

That evening (as far as I can reconstruct it) he transcribed in a fairly ordered, neutral fashion what Foxborough had said out on the terrace, and what it had led to. In a handwriting so different it might almost belong to another person, he then put down the names 'Foxborough and Annamaria' and heavily underlined them both, as if they formed a subheading for what was to follow. But what actually followed was the draft of a poem which he subsequently struck through with a single, disgusted scrawl.

*

SCORING

Like forwards making for the goal-line,
the strings take up the motif, one by one,
and race (with pumping arms and chins tucked in)
towards the gross and grand finale;
the rest of them — woodwinds, timpani,
and now the brass, at last — in loud pursuit.
They're almost there; and I don't give a hoot.
For them the thrill of being just about to come — !
But I'm crocked now: chucked out the game.

*

Leaving barely the space of a single empty line after this abandoned attempt at a poem, he then returned to the subject of Foxborough and Annamaria, and from that to other, related subjects. The whole entry amounts in fact to by far the longest sustained piece of writing he did. Or the longest which survived, anyway.

*

Usually (though not tonight) F is silent in her company – wh is unlike him. He sits forward stiffly in his chair – also a novelty. His eyes lose that self-protective, self-absorbed indifference of theirs. Even his voice changes when he speaks directly to her: it becomes lighter, sweeter (if you please!), more youthful.

He makes no effort to hide his infatuation. She makes no effort to hide the pleasure this gives her. Not a blush but a kind of darkness comes to her skin. Also something like a faint tilt or squint comes into her eyes. Her accent grows a little stronger: more of a Greek roll & emphasis comes into it.

The only other Greeks I've ever really been in contact with were the ones who ran those corner shops in Bloemfntn & C Town, & their wives & kids who also served behind the counter. (Cigarettes & tinned fruit on shelves behind; sweets in those tiered, curved glass cases in front.) Their eyes & brows were dark like hers. Annamaria wd not appreciate the comparison. (Racism!) From a different class she is: governess-educated, wealthy (it seems), refined, self-assured. Delicate hands; clear features; flesh modelled to the bones with a curious exactness; no excess whatever. Eyes: wide-set. Complexion: dark & pale at once. Age: mid-thirties, I'd guess. Marital status: divorced. One child, apparently living with father, wherever he may be. Profession – ? Manner: schoolmarmish. Yet also 'experienced', i.e. intensely alert to men, watchful of them, never showing surprise at anything they do. She somehow even manages to let old Hadison, with his tremendous Roman nose & long white fringe floating around his bald brown nut, have the benefit of her know-ingness. Whereupon booming (ho-ho-ho) & face-wiping & tummy-shaking sets in. And takes a long time to subside.

But she shows no interest in yours truly. I'm excluded. D's word abt me (and my 'condition') in her ear? F's word, via D? God knows.

She & D have apparently known each other for some time. Just recently they've become much closer. It won't last. It wdn't last even if circs were more propitious. D is always collecting (& swapping) 'best friends' (female). The last friend drifts away & a new one arrives. Yet it's kiss-kiss & cries of pleasure whenever any of the earlier ones show up.

I'm the one who stays. Who can't leave. Circe-like, she's put a spell on me. She's turned me not into a pig but into a worm. My soul is wormlike, patently. My prick *is* a worm, nothing else: soft, wiggly, quite incapable of ever standing up for itself. 6 times a day I tell myself not to blame her. 600 times a day I blame her.

And F – what abt him? Think of him as Circe's boss. Or Circe's sorcerer . . . If I cd get my tongue around those 2 words 600 times in succession, without stumbling once, perhaps I'll have discovered the charm to set me free.

Anyhow, that's how he carries on in Annamaria's presence, & she in his. Only I've left out the intensity & brazenness of the proceedings. The fact that they go at it in silence for the most part merely makes it worse. Neither of them gives a damn for anyone else. Why shd they? Who is there for them to give a damn abt? Scowling Tom & his boring Birgit? Terence & friend, off on their own? Hadison? His perky spouse Clara, head to one side, to show how alert she is, what a good sport she is. (You know your joke's a failure if she's the first to titter at it.) Old Mrs F, drifting away into those flat, bare, spectral spaces where very old people seem to go, before they vanish entirely? Me, of all people? D? – ½-pretending it isn't happening; ½-pretending she doesn't care. With childish hurt & self-blame underneath.

Naturally this fills me with *Schadenfreude*. Serves her right, let her suffer etc. Yet, because she's slighted, betrayed, shown up, or feels herself to be so, I feel slighted & betrayed too. Inevitably.

F truly doesn't care abt her now, whatever he may have felt years & years ago. All that effort & intensity, those decisions made & unmade . . . For this!

It still amazes me, looking back, that it shd have taken just one meeting at some bloody theatre – after a couple of yrs of not seeing her, mind you – & what happens? The same old turmoil as ever. This. That. Immediately. She was just a few paces away. She saw me and her expression changed. Neither of us moved. There! She was real! She was mine! The same relief and incredulity as in the old days. Or perhaps I should say: she was *not* mine. Not a thought in my head, you see, but a reality outside it, in the world, self-moving. Therefore always astonishing, never-to-be-known, ever-to-be-discovered.

I was done for. So goodbye Dr Fainman. Thanks for your help.

I can't even remember the play I'd gone to see that night. And why shd she have chosen to patronise it the same evening? Especially in the company of that strange brother of hers, who looks so unlike her I cdn't believe it when she told me who he was. All wounded irony & a rather grand voice: that was his style. Flattish features, a darkish skin. With the red-blue abrasion of a birthmark on the cheekbone & temple, just beneath & above the right eye, seemingly spread over the eye, & a pale, steadfast gaze piercing through. His lips looked as if they'd been turned inside out, from inside: oriental somehow, like in the portrait of a samurai. Hair brushed back sleekly.

Before she was able to introduce us, he went off to get a drink. So I asked her if he was her 'latest'. She looked at me as if I was mad. Again: done for.

I must have walked around for hours afterwards – the West End, Victoria, Pimlico, Battersea – a half-crazed, melodramatic ramble. During it I decided 2 important things: (a) that I loved being in London; & (b) that I cdn't separate any of it from her, neither the parts we'd been in together nor the parts we hadn't. I'd thought of her everywhere. Millions of other people lived there too, which was one of the things I loved abt it: the whole turbid mass & mess of it; its lights & shelves of darkness; its whole geography of bays, creeks, coves, inlets, promontories shaped & scoured by everything that went on inside them or even over them – as the planes did, sighing & whistling, winking with one eye & another, showing perspectives for us to see, not the people inside them; along with noise & stink, bricks & glass, bouncing lorries & crowds moving together, every soul there ignoring

154

& ignored by the neighbours who shared the inside of a bus or a downward-sliding escalator. You – I mean, I – had to love the place for all of this. And Diana at the heart of it. Its woman. Always there. Like the years she'd had ahead of me, always there.

Therefore I had to get out. Break the spell. Try my luck elsewhere: the further away, the better.

No one can say I didn't try to put up a fight. Having Fainman in my corner hadn't helped. Still, that had been one try. Canada (!) was another. How far cd I run? All the way to Toronto apparently. Eventually. Right into the safety of the insurance trade.

Plenty of Greeks in Toronto too, come to think of it. Where behold another vision came unto this displaced Vrystater & Boereseun. O mama. Wat soek hy hier? (Actually it was somewhere upstate New York; but that doesn't matter.) Daar staan hy, the stupid sod, in a field behind a gimcrack shopping plaza, on the outskirts of a nameless town, watching a high-school football game. The teams have turned up in cars bedecked with streamers; other cars stand side by side, facing inwards, windshields bulging like eyes. A brass band bangs & pumps away. Girls in short skirts scream & dance, with much brandishing of pom-poms. The game starts, stops, starts, stops. The players look barely human in their gear; they're moronically, heroically self-important when they take off bits of it. Everything's abstract, disembodied, like an imitation of something else; what, I can't guess. The sky darkens over North America. My own fixed, *a priori* notions not of what I am but of what I shd be and shd feel and shd make of myself suddenly dwindle to nothing. Zero. Where do such ideas come from? Why do we cling to them with such tenacity? Or they to us? The picture I'd had of myself made me believe that my love for ageing Diana, my obsession with the past I cd never share with her, were freakish, distorted, my true self twisted awry. Hence anger & fear, flight, the calling-in of Dr Fainman with his therapeutic powers, flight again to this particular place. Or no place.

155

Bullshit!

It was me. I was whatever it was. That twist *was* my true self. A freak of that sort was what I was intended to be.

In the eye of history etc. it was all an utterly trivial, private business. No doubt. It wd contribute nothing to the fate of nations. (Yet the fate of a nation – my nation – had contributed something tortuous to it, in bringing me there. And D's nation had done its bit for her. If we can't say where anything begins, then who's to say what the end will be? How can you tell?)

Anyway, this, it, us, was as close as I wd ever come to being fated; to having a fate.

So there.

The very point of having a fate is *not* that you know what's going to happen to you, as people imagine, but precisely that you don't. I was the man whose fate had manifested itself by way of a scrambled act of adultery on a sitting-room floor. Now it was showing itself again, under that mucky sky, at the back of that tatty shopping centre, while the game went on & the lights in the distance grew sharper & more forlorn with every darkening moment. If it was my fate to be the shadow-man, as Dr F had said, the absent-present creep, the Johnny-come-afterwards – then so be it. That condition was more intense than anything else I'd ever known.

Not that I jumped on the next plane home (!) (?) Why shd I rush back to England? I had to work off my notice to that insurance co. Also I wanted to travel abt the States. Deliberate, that's what I made up my mind to be. No rushing this time. No fear. (In both senses.) The mess I was going back to wd wait patiently for me. It was my mess, after all. My fate.

EIGHTEEN

On he went. He could not stop. The longer he sat at the task the more intensely and the more rapidly he wrote. Or so the appearance of these pages suggests. His writing tilted, rushed, sprawled. Every now and again the words are punctuated by tiny, angry stars, splutters of lead, where the point of his pencil broke; so hard was he pressing on it.

*

Just abt a week after getting back from the States: to the F house once again – walking there from the tube station, as on previous visits. Autumn; evening; flapping winds; gusts of rain; trees in commotion; leaves coming down one after the other. Panic-stricken passengers dropping off a wrecked ship. Once fallen, though, the leaves stuck like glue to the paving. Passing headlights making everything silver that wasn't black; in the after-dazzle, streaks of bruise-like colour swimming & struggling among the raindrops.

There was the wooden gate in front of the house; there, the path. The shadows on it shook & pointed; irritably brushed away by the wind, as if by a mad housewife, they always returned.

Now, the door & doorbell.

It was only the 4th time I'd rung that bell; each time in such different circumstances. And yet again.

D opened the door. We hadn't seen each other after that meeting at the theatre, almost a year before. We'd spoken only once on the phone, since my return. A long, agitated call it was, on my side at any rate; she confined mostly to Mm's and Oh's and Well's – of various kinds – understanding, reproving, tired, pleased, nervous, doubtful. A lot of the last especially.

157

I said to her, 'Well, I've come.'

F appeared behind her, in the half-lit hall. He was wearing a sweater, neat collar, tie.

I looked from one to the other. So did D. So did F. Nobody spoke.

D made up her mind suddenly. 'Come in.' It sounded like a command, not an invitation. Getting it over with.

The furniture in the living-room had been rearranged since I was last there. That's what I noticed. The armchairs & couch which had been in the bay were now in the main body of the room; in the bay was a dining-table with some chairs around it. I was the first to go in. The others followed.

F: 'You weren't expecting to see me.'

Me: 'No.' Long pause.

Now D's turn: 'I've told Rodney about you.'

Still her turn: 'And me.'

Then, with even more of an effort: 'I did it ages ago. It was after we'd stopped seeing each other. I had to do it then – I don't know why. Rodney told me he'd known all about us, all the time.'

'Oh.' I began to tremble. I cdn't help it. After a dim, strange lapse, something going through the three of us that wasn't only time passing, I asked, 'Should I leave?'

F: 'No. You should sit down.'

Which I did.

What followed was one of his performances. One of his best.

Only the word 'performance' gives the wrong idea: as if he'd worked it all out beforehand. It's not like that. Never is. Wasn't even on that occasion. You can see he relishes his own words, all right; but it's as if that's partly because he doesn't know where they're going to lead him. Manner detached yet attentive; self-absorbed but curious. Voice steady; gaze unflinching & unseeing.

Off he went then. 'After years of marriage you're bound to take your partner for granted. People say that's a bad thing to do. But it means that you also take for granted

158

loyalty, privacy, truth-telling. Then you discover that you've been exposed to disloyalty & lies.'

Since D didn't speak, I did. 'You could have told us that you knew.'

'Yes. And you could have told me what you were up to. Either of you. Both of you. You chose not to. So I did – no, not the same, but something like the equivalent. Neither of you is in a position to reprove me for it.'

'No.'

'Very well then. How was I to react? Like Othello? I've always detested him, with his whining & braggadocio. Try to be Christian & forgiving? Difficult if you're not Christian & not especially forgiving by nature. Start blaming myself: it's my fault, I too have sinned, it's not for me to accuse others? A possibility, I suppose, but not an appealing one. Curiosity – prurient or otherwise? Also a possibility. Indifference, too. Or what about a renewed sexual interest in my wife, who was still capable, apparently, of exciting someone else?'

We sat there like chidden children. He listened to his own words – as he uttered them, and after each lot of phrases too – dark head turned slightly to one side. When D tried to speak he held up his hand, not angrily, as if to say, 'My turn now.'

'And that's not all, by any means. There were other possibilities. Disbelief, for example. I mean by that *you*' – & it was as if he unhooded his eyes to stare at me. A moment later, with not even a blink to mark the change, his gaze was as expressionless as before. 'Also dislike of being seen as a gullible fool, of course, by you or by the people to whom you no doubt told your precious secret.

'The really devilish part of it, though, is that all these alternatives are not alternatives at all; they're simultaneities, co-existents. They're plainly incompatible with one another; & yet you find that it's possible to feel all of them at the same time – or would be if you allowed yourself to do it. The lot, from Othello-like rage to stark indifference. And fatigue. As well as an amazing impulse to applaud. "Good for Diana, we only live once etc.!"'

'I sometimes wondered if I'd ever hear from her about it.' Only the pronoun, not the direction of his eyes, showed he was again addressing me, not us both. 'Is there a statute of limitations in such matters? I doubt it. The lies & silences of the past can't be recuperated. Nor can any of us pick up where we left off.

'What's it now – three years? – more? – since you were last . . . attached? That's a long time. A very long time. Diana assured me when she made her confession that she had no interest whatever in renewing the affair. I believed her then & I believe her now. *A fortiori* now. Especially after seeing you.'

We sat in our places, neither of us looking at the others. Throughout D had kept her head lowered, her hands in her lap. She was subdued but unabashed, speechless, composed.

F spoke again. 'She also tells me that you've turned up babbling about her being your fate, & so on.' He gave me the benefit of his gaze again. The maleficence of it, rather. 'So how do you intend to live out your fate now? Or will you try to manage without it? Find a new one, perhaps?'

'No.'

'What do you mean? You don't plan to carry her away by force, do you?'

'No. I've got no plans. No expectations. I came back because – I had to. I'll stay with her, I'll be her friend for ever, if she'll let me. And yours too, if you'd allow me to.'

Silence, a long one, while F considered the matter. Or appeared to.

'Done!' he said.

Done & done.

Many surprises lay ahead; the gtst surprise – no! the 2nd gtst surprise – being the *speed* of time's passing. Anyone wd think that the lapse of 6 years must feel, in retrospect at least, like half a lifetime gone by. It's almost as long a period, after all, as the one betwn leaving C Town and finishing my pupillage; longer than the time I spent in senior school. All that went on for ever, or seemed to – full of eddies & runs & backwashes & stagnant pools of time. Now the years flicker past in a daze, in a distracted glide. Seasons come & go much as I imagine they do for old Mrs F, say: each day long enough, more than long enough; but each year hardly more than the wink of an eye, of no consequence except for the knowledge that it's been & that it's not going to recur.

I tell myself: look how lucky you are! I've got this career in the civil service – one I never expected to follow, OK, but I've 'never looked back' as they say, since it began. Definitely not looked back at the bar. Struggling for briefs, trying to beat my own path through the profession – no thanks. Not in the state I was in when I came back from Canada. I hadn't the spunk for it. The blessed safety of the civil service (admin grade, please sir) was an irresistible lure. Even being an outsider hasn't been nearly the drawback at work I'd thought it might be. (If anything colleagues sometimes feel freer with me than they do with each other, in their creepy, tentacular English fashion.) So – I've got my work; my flat; my friends, male and female – as well as this friendship, & something more, with the F's; my 'project' on F's life & work; my other bits of writing; my English-type appetite for gossip which surprises & slightly disgusts me; the chance to travel; my love for the opera (the lusher the better); plus the money to indulge myself in it, here & abroad.

So see me in the stalls with wet eyes and a heaving breast, like many another sentimental bachelor.

There – lucky! Take a look at it from the back streets of Bloemfontein and say it again: lucky!

Up to a point.

Let's assume my old Freudian friend was right abt the Primal Scene etc. For the sake of argument, say yes, it happened, it was a big deal. What he left out is that that Scene did not make me what I am; rather, *what I am made it important to me.* I'm the one who seized on it.

The same cd be said abt any such explanatory, cause-finding

161

interpretation of my own or anyone else's behaviour. Recognition is quite another matter: not at all the same thing as interpretation. It disrupts the frameworks that interpretation depends on – psycho-analytical, religious, whatever they may be. Recognition speaks to us from inside our fantasies. It says, *That's* what you can be. *This* can matter more to you than anything else. *Here's* yr chance to experience what you're afraid of. *Now* you can find out what you really want. And all this with no guarantees as to how things will work out; indeed, the very opposite; risk & fear at the heart of it.

Mystical gibberish? No. In none of my fantasies did I dream of becoming a civil servant. Nor did I dream of becoming, in my private life, a servant of quite another kind: a well-trained, sympathetic, indispensable houseboy.

That does not make the fantasies that shaped me, provoked me, brought me to England, stuck me to D, and so forth, any the less mine; or my present state any the less their perverse fulfilment. Perversity was presumably always a part of them. As in some malign fairy tale, my wishes, or a simulacrum of them, have been granted to me. Now, just like the deluded heroes of such tales, I have to pay the price for having made these wishes in the first place.

Loss of pride, for one thing. Loss of independence, for another. Loss of manhood, worst of all.

Six years of it!

They tell me that the word 'houseboy' is never used these days by the liberals back in S Africa. Houseboys still abound there, of course. It seems to me that I've become a local, specialised version of the species. The rewards I get are the ones usually given to 'good' houseboys: they become trusted confidants & counsellors, positively friends of the family.

In dreams, no problem; no difficulty in getting it up & getting it in. (Though even the best of them nowadays, the happiest, the fiercest, are infiltrated by daylight anxieties, so that in the middle of grappling with the wonderfully pliant, co-operative females summoned up for me, by me, I'm half-comically beset by voices – my own voice – saying, *Look it's easy, I can do it, where's the problem?*)

But before, afterwards, awake . . . I'm still bewildered (after all this time) by what's happened.

By what doesn't happen. Where it's gone.

All the sights & thoughts – let alone the actions, feelings, touches – wh used to set me going, wh I *relied* on to get me going, wh I took for granted wd always work – simply no longer have the power to do it. Or perhaps it's truer to say that I don't have the power to respond to them.

It's quite uncanny; interesting too, in a way. I think the thoughts, or touch the flesh, & instead of the consequences being the ones positively *owing* to me – nothing.

Or at best a faint, archival stirring.

The will can't help you here; all it ever does is lead you from one fiasco to another. I've been through some pretty ones. Ugly ones too. And it's no help that it's all the standard subject of jokes in pubs & on tv screens.

Quite the reverse. And as for those serious articles in the 'serious' papers – !

In the end the whole female race, with their hair & dresses, legs & bosoms, soft skins & secret places, becomes a kind of unspoken, unadmitted reproach to you.

Not that they wd know it. Or perhaps they do. *Vide*, the wide-awake Annamaria.

The tricks you get up to! (I, I, I, for God's sake – not a mythical, neutral 'you'.) Convinced of the inevitability of failure ahead, I don't avoid the company of women these days; anything but; instead I warn them, delicately, pre-emptively, of 'problems' in this area. The upshot? I've become the big expert in elaborate flirtations which never go anywhere. Complete with outings to the opera, intimate dinners, sighs & silences suggestive of grievous disappointment in the past. Plus of course gossip abt this one and that, him, her, and them.

A substitute gratification. The eunuch's wank.

The amazing & depressing thing is how many women there are who are willing to do a deal on these terms: women

163

who love other people's problems, or who have intractable problems of their own, or both.

One thing I'm not prepared to do, however, is to go back to Dr Feigning. Nor am I interested in finding a Feigning substitute. Which doesn't stop me from browsing among those shelves in bookshops where paperbacks on sexual & other health problems are piled high. Give me that 'hypno-therapy' man! How abt a dose of yr 'rejuvenation treatment', sweetheart? Chiefly I just go on hoping for the best; waiting for something to happen, for something to change, to meet a woman who'll set me free.

Not D. She's part of the problem not part of the solution, as those self-loving, long-haired radical craps like to say.

The question of our becoming lovers again doesn't arise. We're on quite another footing now. She's my closest friend & I'm hers: that's how it is, that's how it's going to stay. Since we now see each other publicly as well as privately, it sometimes seems to me we have even more to talk abt than we used to, in the good old days. Having been so intimate we can afford to expose our vulnerabilities to one another. I tell her abt my 'difficulties' & the tortuous alliances & negotiations that follow. What wd I have done all this time without her sympathetic ear to confide in? She tells to me abt her unhappiness at home, with T & husband, the one as much as the other. I've been led stage by stage, e.g. through the saga of T's trying to get into university, wh went on for a long time; then of his dropping out of it, wh happened overnight; then of his eventual departure for Paris – ostensibly to learn French, with the ultimate intention, he claimed, of becoming a journalist. Now there's his return with friend, having become not a journalist, it seems, but an avowed homosexual: gtly to Mama's distress & self-blame. (Though she also feels that she shdn't either show it or – something much more difficult to accomplish – feel it.) As for F – she complains abt his moodiness, selfishness, indifference to her wishes. In return, like the beloved houseboy I've become, I give her my own, reassuring impression of the master's needs & states of mind.

For am I not F's friend & confidant too, now? Don't we have our own relationship? Haven't I been allowed to rummage through his papers; to hear his reminiscences of Finland & of his time at Oxford; to speak to him abt his first wife; to pick up from him the latest gossip emanating from the BBC?

You bet. Of course my exchanges with F are not as deep, nowhere near as easy, as those with D. Still –

Still –

She's putting on weight, undeniably. (So'm I.) It shows in her face especially. (Mine too.) Her cheeks are beginning to sink down on both sides of her lips. (Not true of me, hooray.) The lines that run down into her chin grow deeper as a result. She's more careless than she used to be abt her hair, & the colour that shows under the gilding is not the mousy shade I used to study at such close quarters with nose & fingers & eyes; it's distinctly grey. And of course specs for reading now: large, hornrimmed ones that give her an implausibly intellectual air.

As in the old days, though for different reasons, we touch each other hardly at all in public. In private we're both more guarded and less so: I don't know how else to describe it. When we do touch she's always the initiator. Her caresses are never passionate, merely affectionate. I respond by touching back (places I've been to, long ago), by smiling, by looking at her; never more than that. Occasionally we marvel at how things have 'worked out'. Who'd ever have thought when we were lovers that a relationship like this wd some day be possible for us – one so easy – & enduring – & without recrimination & embarrassment . . . ?

It's mostly D who says such things; I'm the one who just agrees with them. Yes, it is amazing. No, of course I don't blame her for my 'difficulties'. (Abt wh she's invariably reassuring. The main thing is for me not to worry: it happens to most men at one time or another: it'll come right: who knows better than she does just what I'm capable of in that line? Smile, lowered head.) I tell her I'll never forget what she's been to me & how much I owe to her. She transformed me, I say, from the naïve, callow, blundering provincial I was into – what I am now.

Poor D! How distant the days when I thought of her as the incarnation of everything metropolitan & off-hand, sportive & inscrutable. When I tell her she's the one who's made me what I am, she actually takes it as a compliment. It's incredible & pitiable. She simply doesn't register the tone of voice in wh I say such things.

The hatred in it.

Our conversations resemble those fantasies I used to nourish when I was her lover, & wd imagine myself telling some other woman abt our affair, long after it was over. What I'd gained from it, what I'd suffered in it, and so forth. The one thing I never dreamed of then was that the attentively listening woman at the other end wd turn out to be, of all people, Diana herself!

Eternally Diana. Unshakably Diana. Beloved, hated, fated Diana.

She still does mad things. The other day, when we were in that tea-room above the sea, and that waitress was so rude to her, she took one of the Cornish cream pastries from the tray on the table, opened it up, stuck a gt dollop of mustard into the middle of it, closed it again, and replaced it innocently in the tray. I pointed out that the person who'd suffer wd be the next poor sod of a customer who bit hopefully into it, but she wasn't bothered. 'It'll give the place the bad name it deserves to have.' And that was that. We drank our tea & left. No tip. Just an exchange of glares between her & the waitress.

He is determined to get rid of her. I haven't the slightest doubt of it. Annamaria is now the one in his life. It's decided, settled in his mind, I can see it. Annamaria's mind doesn't matter so much. She'll give way to him, gladly. I can see that too.

I said this to Diana before I left this evening. Simply: 'He's determined to get rid of you.' She made no reply. I said, 'What will you do then?' She opened her eyes wide. As always, I felt myself drawn into them; I cd have wandered for a month in their spoilt depths; there I'd rediscover everything about her which I'd supposedly forgotten. No words from her; so – none from me.

I was on the point of leaving when she said:

'Then I'll have nobody but you.'

NINETEEN

He had intended to go back to Sandarac for dinner, hours before. Instead he had remained in his room, at the table, pencil in hand, filling page after page of the wire-bound exercise book in front of him. Some biscuits from a packet and a can of soft drink had been enough to sustain him. Twice he had made a journey to the lavatory, down the dark passage outside, conscious of the breathing, sleeping Merrimans behind closed doors – parents, children, with whom he would be making conversation at breakfast.

Now the task he had set himself was finished. Breakfast was barely more than three or four hours away. The sky was alive with the changes bringing in the day. There had always been a rich, purplish hue to the night, moonless though it had been; now it was tinged with green as well, from end to end. All along the eastern horizon what was curved and tinted was disengaging itself from the flat blackness beneath it. Soon a lighter colour still, a kind of yellowing, showed itself there.

Impossible to sleep. So he stayed at the window. The song of invisible birds rose to a clamour and then subsided. Objects of all kinds slowly separated themselves from each other, as the sky and earth had already done: first the larger (hedge from field; shed from house; tree from tree); then those that were smaller and smaller still, until even individual wires and blades of grass could clearly be made out. It was as if they had spent the night merged in one another's arms and were only now, like lovers, turning aside, putting space between themselves, looking out at the day. Long before the sun had risen there was a sourceless, shadeless light everywhere, strong enough to have given colour to everything.

Then he went to bed and slept for a couple of hours.

*

Later that morning he, Diana, Foxborough, Annamaria, and Clara Hadison drove to the coast. They took with them their bathing costumes, towels, a blanket, and a thermos flask of tea. In the little port nearest to Sandarac they went to a boatyard and hired for the day a small boat, a fourteen-footer with an outboard motor. This was Annamaria's idea; it was her (expensive) treat, her way of making up to Foxborough for his disappointment on hearing from Tom, earlier in the morning, that he was still not satisfied with the reliability of the motor of the clumsy boat at home.

So in this hired boat, with Foxborough at the wheel, they set out along the coast. The weather was good and not expected to change – they had listened to the forecast on the radio before leaving – and the sea was calm. The tide was on the turn. There was no cloud in the sky; only a high, even haze that blurred and enlarged the disc of the sun, seeming to intensify its heat and diffuse its glare to every corner of the sky. The haze made the sea look almost brownish in the distance; but nearby it was black, white, pale green, anything. It came against the hull of the boat with a slap and a splash, and again, and again, sportively, even domestically, and hissed and skidded away each time, as if across the surface of itself, over the wrinkling and writhing that went on below. There were a few other craft out: bigger ones with day-trippers; motor-boats like their own, some occupied by fishermen and their rods; a couple of small sailing boats. Out at sea bigger ships stood off, seeming to make no progress at all, despite the smoke that trailed from them in vague, flat streamers, which broadened out before they vanished. With a mere swing of its own weight the water again and again struck against fractured cliff-faces and fallen rock to the right; on the beaches its breakers appeared to be no more than playful tumblers, somersaulters, eager dashers at nothing, like the children here and there who ran shouting in and out of them.

Foxborough hummed to himself, his blue windcheater zipped up to the neck, locks of his hair jumping and flying about. Their trousered knees touching, three of the passengers sat on the U-shaped bench just behind him. For lack of space Clara had gone into the little cabin in front: not because she was the smallest of them, but because she was the most self-deprecating, and because the crouching and bending necessary to get in there, and to stay there, enabled her to show how keen she was. Then she could stick her cropped grey head out of the door and grin back at the others – which she did, all the way.

Annamaria wore a jaunty blue cap, like a Russian schoolboy's; Diana had tied her hair with a scarf knotted under her chin. Behind it the boat left a little wake and a smell of combustion, both lost in an instant.

*

It was Diana who insisted that they put in at that particular cove. Passing it, seeing it again, she remembered it from when she was a girl. She and her brother and sister used to go there with her parents; they had always thought of it as a secret, special place. When the tide was low you could walk there from 'next door', as she put it; it was also quite safe to approach it from the sea, which they had done many times. The beach was sandy, clear, hazard-free. They would easily be able to find a landing place. With a boat as small as this there was no problem in beaching it; they could simply swing up the motor and then push it off when it was time to go.

Foxborough was not persuaded. He wanted to stick to the destination they had had in mind on setting out: a place they had visited previously by car, further along the coast, where there were proper moorings on a small breakwater. There was also beach there and a path going up to a tea-room and a pub nearby. Above the noise of the idling motor, and of the idling, rocking water, husband and wife bickered briefly; their guests sat in silence, Clara still trapped inside, Annamaria trailing her hand over the side, turning her wrist this way and that in the cold, busy water.

Finally Foxborough said, 'Very well then. If you really want to stay here I'll drop off you and Adrian.'

'Fine,' Diana assented. 'Then you can come and pick us up later. Bags us the thermos and the blanket.'

170

None of them commented on Foxborough's manner of pairing them off. Cautiously he turned the boat into the cove, with Annamaria looking behind them, to make sure the propeller did not foul itself in the sand. When she gave the word, just a few yards from the beach, the debarking pair took off their shoes, rolled up the legs of their trousers, and, with more lurches and wobbles than anyone had bargained for, let themselves over the side. They were handed the basket and a carrier bag with the blanket and flask, their towels and costumes.

Having waded ashore, they waved from the beach to the pair on the boat.

'One o'clock,' Diana yelled, pointing at her watch and then holding up a single finger, and Annamaria nodded and pointed at hers. Foxborough turned the boat around without difficulty. Clara began to clamber out of her hutch. Annamaria waved her hand at them as the boat disappeared around the headland.

*

At any rate that is the story my friend told me. It is the one he told the coroner too. Foxborough's story, like Annamaria's, and Clara's, was different. They had understood Diana to say that she and her companion would spend some time in the cove and then walk back to the harbour from which they had set out. There was no problem about getting to the cliff-top walk from the next cove. Whichever party arrived at the starting-point would wait for the others to return.

Clearly, the coroner said, a tragic misunderstanding had taken place; one made all the more unfortunate by the fact that Mr Foxborough had obviously relied on his wife's superior knowledge of the coastline and of local conditions, which derived from the time she had spent in the area during her youth.

Lies, said my friend. Foxborough had misunderstood nothing. He knew what Diana had said and what she was expecting him to do. He knew what the tides were like on that coast. He did not care. He had dismissed her. That was his way. His gift. There were more important things on his mind: Annamaria for one. How he must have cursed being stuck with Clara, once he had seen how things had worked out! But they got rid of her, anyway; they abandoned her in the tea-room, while they sneaked off together for a good couple of hours, like a pair of adolescents. Diana could fend for herself, and if she failed to do so – too bad. The same went for her fancy man, or ex-fancy man.

And Annamaria? Was she guilty too?

Of course! She did not give a damn either. She would say and do anything Foxborough told her to. It would never occur to her to contradict him. The only thing that could be said in her favour was that she had not visited Cornwall before and might not have realised beforehand what was at stake. Once the catastrophe had happened, however, she had not only Foxborough to protect but also her belief in her own innocence. No doubt it had taken her seconds merely to believe that Foxborough's version of events was correct, and to forget what she, Annamaria, her hand over the side of the boat, wrist-deep in the water, had actually heard. Then it was settled; the two of them were agreed, innocent; headstrong Diana herself, not to mention her stupid friend, were to blame for what had occurred.

As for Clara – she was just a joke. Stuck in that cucumber-frame of a cabin she had heard nothing at all. Only impudence and sycophancy had made her claim otherwise.

*

It was peaceful in the cove. Their arrival had been watched by another couple there; but they soon left, making their way through the fallen rock on the eastern side of the cove, and so out of sight.

Breakers sighed hoarsely and rippled against the sand. Among the rocks they made more vehement noises. Louder and softer than these, yet another sound hung in the air: something continuous and unchanging, a single note which seemed to derive not from movement but from an unimaginable stillness.

They spread out their blanket so that half of it was in the diffuse sunlight, half in the shade of a rock projecting from the cliff-face. Behind that rock Diana got into her bathing costume, neither hiding from him nor displaying herself; he caught a

172

glimpse of one pale, dark-tipped breast swaying, pointing down-wards; and a shimmy of her belly as she crammed herself into the bottom of her two-piece costume, above straining white legs. She was going straight into the sea, she said, and teased him for being so 'feeble' in not joining her. 'If you don't do it now you'll never do it.'

But having changed into her costume, she lay on the blanket with him. On her stomach, chin on her fist, legs sprawled in a V, she told him about a 'stupid' argument she had had with Foxborough at breakfast; a kind of a continuation, she supposed, of the equally stupid discussion they had had the previous evening about 'historic' and 'non-historic' peoples. This one had started because Foxborough had come to the table claiming that the number of non-English people in the party (a Greek, a German, and an Afrikaner) had to be 'statistically significant'. 'Significant of what?' Diana had asked; and in his most infuriating manner he answered, 'Can't you guess?' No, she said, she couldn't. To which, in the presence of Annamaria, Birgit, and his mother, he said that in that case she was even more stupid than he had supposed.

'What did he mean? What's it supposed to reveal about us? Is it meant to be a good thing or a bad one? Whatever I asked him he sneered at. In any case, what can statistics be worth when the group is so small?' Diana now asked, like an earnest student hoping for a reply; and her companion was surprised to see tears spring into her eyes. She was not a weeper; that was one of the things about her he had noticed early in their acquaintance.

(Was this unpleasant marital exchange at breakfast evidence that should have been given to the coroner? Or her recounting of it later?)

'Why does it upset you so much?'

'Because he despises me. He makes gnomic remarks like that in order to show me up. He knows I'll rise to them, like a sucker. I always do. It's become a habit on both sides. And of course it's worse than ever now he's got someone else. Or is getting someone else. Or thinks he's getting someone else.'

173

They were both silent. Then he said: 'He's a tease. I don't really understand him, but that's one thing I'm sure of. Maybe there's less about him to understand than I've ever supposed.'

Later, looking at the shining, tireless sea, they talked again about God: her God. The argument she put forward that day (it changed every time the subject came up between them) went like this. If the earth was nothing more than a speck of dust floating in infinite space, and we ourselves nothing more than unimaginably minuscule dust-mites floating and fucking on it, we were these things only because we had the capacity to think of ourselves in such terms. Infinite space and time – and the selfhood of each of us too – existed only so far as we were conscious of them.

'Well? All you're doing when you talk like that is repeating Pascal – more or less,' he objected. 'You know, man is a reed, but at least he's a thinking reed. That doesn't tell us anything about God.'

'No, it does. You can't have a consciousness which doesn't belong to someone: to something like a person. Right? There's no such thing as a non-personal consciousness. Nor can there be a consciousness anywhere that isn't conscious of itself. It has to *belong* to someone. A self.'

'So?'

'We're also conscious of each other, aren't we?'

'Yes.'

'So why shouldn't there be a consciousness beyond ours, which is conscious of us – as we are of mites, say – as well as of itself; and another one beyond that? And yet another after that . . . ? If we can think of space being infinite, or time, why can't we think of consciousness, or maybe consciousness*es*, being infinite too? We can't actually picture infinity, I know, but the idea of it is part of us, not just in maths or physics, but in everything we think and feel about ourselves. It's the same with an infinite consciousness. I can't picture it or imagine it but I know it's there. The idea of it is part of me. I'm conscious of it, like I'm conscious of infinite space, or of time being endless. So I must be a part of it too, as I am of space or time. Nothing is entirely lost. Not this. Not me. Not you.'

174

'What a terrible idea. It's a comfort to think of things being lost.'

'You lie,' she answered hotly. 'You! You hate losing even what was never yours.'

Then, his ears filled with the sound which was not a sound, which came from nowhere and everywhere, he fell asleep.

*

He dreamed that there were large bricks in front of him, almost a wall of them, unstable-seeming, made out of some light, rough material like fibre-glass. They were a source of radiant, unquenched warmth. Every one of them could be opened like a box in a safe-deposit vault. This was a secret known only to him. But the whole thing might tumble down if he tried to do it.

He woke up before it happened. He did not know where he was. The sky was the same as before, only more glaring. That was where the warmth in his dream had come from. In that moment, remembering the warmth, he remembered the dream and recognised what was around him: sand, rocks, the noise of the sea, Diana standing above him. She had put on her blouse, over her costume-top. He said, by way of excuse, 'I hardly slept at all last night.' Then, 'I was having an idiotic dream. I may have come into a fortune in the middle of it, but I couldn't be sure.' He looked at his watch and sat up. 'Good God, it's long past one already. Shouldn't they have come for us by now?'

'I'd have thought they'd be back. But it doesn't matter. They'll show up. I hope so. I'm getting hungry.'

'Let's have tea, anyway.'

Looking at her as she busied herself with the thermos flask, he asked, 'What did you do while I was asleep?'

'Oh, I went into the water for a bit, but it was too cold. Then I lay down too and dozed off for a while. Afterwards I watched you sleeping.'

'That must have been fun.'

'It used to be,' she said sadly.

*

The waves were breaking higher on the beach than before: appreciably so. He sat and watched them for some time; then

175

got up and looked across the swinging waste of light and water out there, forever mounting beyond the local turmoil to the furthest reach of whatever it was that seemed to contain it. A motor-boat went by; not Foxborough's. He felt no anxiety about his absence, however; only irritation.

*

Later Diana said, 'I think we've missed our chance to get out around the side. Perhaps I should have woken you sooner, but I didn't want to disturb you. Anyway, it doesn't matter. Rodney knows we're waiting for him.'

'Well, he'd better show up then, hadn't he?'

'Yes.'

*

'And if he doesn't come?'

'Then we'll yell at someone from another boat.'

'He'll be mad with us when he turns up and finds we're gone.'

'Not half as mad as I'll be with him if he doesn't show up at all.'

'Will he ever know?'

'What?'

'How mad you were with him.'

'Very funny. Very cheerful.'

*

The waves made their endless obeisances to the shrinking beach, then they arched back, tried to withdraw, to struggle out to the open sea. But they were caught each time and sent forward again by the ever-increasing power of the beleaguering spaces behind them. Where the incoming waves met those struggling back, sand and small pebbles rose up as if in a funnel, to be milled and thrown aside. It made a noise like a giant plug being pulled, each time. Further out other waves curved over to begin their charge, showing arched bellies marbled with foam, aswirl with cross-currents; behind each one the advancing water was pulled tight into strands, like colourless hair. Then belly, hair, inside, out, above, below, collapsed in a single white confusion; only for the same to happen to another breaker, and another, fiercer and higher than the last. They were all now striking with

176

a roar and an under-boom against the rocks and the prows of the cliff-face; lashed into white, claw-like reachings and grabbings of foam, they flung themselves away empty-handed and came back avid for more.

'If you ask me we should clear off,' he said. 'We can still make it round the side, don't you think?'

She looked at the lunging water, the flying spray, the drenched, shining rocks which emerged and went under, only to rise racing and streaming again. 'No, we're better off waiting for them. Rodney won't forget. He's not going to leave us here.'

'Are you sure?'

'How can I be?' she said, suddenly angry. 'It's what I think.'

'Are you frightened?'

'Not if you're not.'

'I don't think I am,' he lied.

*

It was different, though, when the mist came down. It settled in suddenly; in a couple of minutes, it seemed. There had been no warning of its coming: only a thickening over the sea that was so slight, initially, it was more like a blurring of their half-dazed vision than a process taking place out there, above the water.

Like a glittering veil, the mist stayed offshore, leaving the beach quite clear, the sun still shining on the rocks and cliff-faces behind them. A few feet above the waves, it swayed and moved forward only with the advancing water. Weightless but grainy it appeared to be, almost flocculent. It seemed to possess a private, fantastical quiet of its own. It would help. It had to be of help to them. But out of it came the same uproar, the ocean's archings, smashings, contractings, sudden swellings and unbelievably rapid spreadings everywhere. With no end or pause to any of it.

'What are we going to do?'

'We should try and make it around those rocks.'

She said: 'Never. I'd rather sit it out up there.'

They eyed the ledge above them, and the pathway going to it; then the breakers rushing out of the mist to savage the rocks and to be savaged by them. Already water rustled and ran at the foot of the cliff, making paths for itself through the sand and rocks there, with little banks and swift tributaries. He went down the crevasse at the centre of the cove to see if there were a pathway through it and beyond it. But there was no way out. It was quieter there; that was all. When he returned to the contracted beach, even smaller now than when he had left it a moment before, the noise struck his ears with redoubled force. He almost staggered under the assault of it; and of the light; and of the uprearing, inlooped walls of water making for him. He could not draw breath before them. Nothing could be seen that was level, nothing still. It was as if the world's stuff was running amok. Only the cliffs rose unyieldingly above. The distant, intimate sound they had heard earlier, that steady undertone and overtone, was gone. The water heaved itself up and moved in many directions at once, it thundered and snarled, it sucked insanely at sand and rock, its spray rising so high to meet the falling spray that all of it seemed to hang motionless up there. Impossible not to think of a murderous purpose in all the turnings and hurryings of the tide, its bridal-white flouncings and lunges; yet they were also hugely headless, witless, inhuman and indifferent, just what they were, would always be.

If only the noise, the flying and heaving, would stop! If only they were given a moment's peace to think! Diana's face was turned to him in fear and incredulity; there was also a flicker on it of a strange embarrassment. She had brought him there. She had exposed him to this. On the sand were their pathetic belongings, a blanket and a towel, no protection for them against anything.

*

Later, drenched already, they climbed the narrow path ascending to the ledge – 'Diana's ledge' was the uncanny name he gave it, in describing to me what happened. There they should have enjoyed a precarious safety from anything but an unusually high tide (which did not occur that day) or from a single, freakishly high wave (which might have occurred at any moment, but did not). Yet that was to take no account of the effects of cold, shock, exhaustion, isolation, the never-ceasing din of the waves they could not look at and could not hide from, the slipperiness of the rock and the shuddering of the blows it received. Their place

178

was wide enough to sit on, sideways on, but no more than that; there were no handholds above it.

He survived the ordeal. Diana did not. After yet another unseen mass of water had crashed against the cliffside below, after yet another screen of water had been thrown up before them and over them and streamed away, he turned his head. Where Diana had been, she was not.

PART FOUR

TWENTY

That was the story he told first to the inquest and then to me: many times. To the end of his life he insisted that responsibility for the death of Diana lay squarely on Foxborough's shoulders. His was the criminal malice or criminal disregard which had brought it about. More than that, perhaps even worse than that: he was convinced that Foxborough was so armoured by conceit and self-control no pangs of guilt or remorse would ever afflict him. Diana's death had gone unavenged; the man who had left her on that beach, who had promised to return to it, who knew the tide was coming in and what it would do if she waited for him there – that man had escaped scot free, even in his own consciousness, from paying a penalty of any kind. So trusting she had been, in waiting for him; and with what result?

Bastard! Killer!

*

We met again, my former pen-pal and I, about four years after Diana's death. He was almost forty by then; I was twenty-five.

Our correspondence had long since lapsed. But it had left us on a different footing with one another from before. Though we had not seen each other for so long, we found ourselves at once, and without any difficulty, on almost intimate terms. It seemed we had to make little effort to recover lost ground, to learn to know each other anew. Had we met while we were actually writing to one another, I suspect this would never have been the case. But no shyness or awkwardness arose. We were old friends at once; lovers not long after.

Once again we met at a party; again it was one given by my brother and his wife. Among all the guests in their finery, among the pictures and gleaming pieces of furniture which our hosts collected, nothing shone so brightly as the faces of their two small children, my nephew and niece. Their hair was lovingly washed and brushed for the occasion; their faces were alight with excitement and pride. They went around ardently offering cocktail snacks on trays they had just enough strength to hold horizontal – the white-shirted boy who is now a surgeon in Australia; his sister sheathed in pale blue satin for the occasion, with a blue Alice-band over her hair, who was some twelve years later to be rescued from starving herself to death in a flat in Holloway.

He had changed, my pen-pal. He was now more than solidly built; he was positively heavy in the jowls as well as his hips. His eyes had lost the clarity I remembered; they even looked darker in hue. His hair was thinner; retreating, it had left more of his freckled, lustreless scalp exposed. Only his voice was exactly the same to my ears: it had a strained, effortful quality, as if it came out through a constricted throat. He roused my curiosity at once.

And something more than that. The glamour of the past we had 'shared' was still on him. It would never leave him. He would always remain one of my brother's mysterious, grown-up friends; to that extent, still nurtured and neglected within me, there lurked the little girl who had known him, the excluded child who had hungered to know more and to be more than she already was.

Yet we were also equals at last. That was what time had done for me.

Let me make it clear: I may have been young when we met again, but I no longer thought of myself as a flapper, a student, an inexperienced woman. I had a job with a weekly journal of economic affairs (where, since I was a linguist of sorts, 'European culture' had somehow become my speciality); I was not friendless or bored or looking for adventures. I had a flat of my own in Clapham; I owed nobody anything at all. It did not take me long to gather that he was in much the same situation. 'Are you married?' I asked him, quite early in our conversation. 'Or anything?'

'Neither married nor anything. And you?'

'Me neither.'

That mutual confession left us feeling slightly constrained for the first time. Then he said, 'I'm nothing.'

'Nothing?' I repeated mockingly, taking my tone from his.

But he did not respond. 'The last time we heard from each other you were still a student. I was in the Home Office. I've chucked that. Now I'm with an outfit called Public Policy Enquiry.'

'The think-tank?'

'You know it?'

'The Tory think-tank?'

'I see you do know it. How come you're so well-informed?'

I told him the name of the journal I worked for. I could see he was impressed. When he heard that I worked on its 'culture' side, however, he was less impressed. 'That's not why people buy the journal, is it?'

'No. But they'd complain if it wasn't there.'

'True.'

'And you? What do you do at your place?'

'Oh, mostly administer. Plan. Try to raise money. Think, sometimes.'

I said to him impulsively, 'Why are you so sad?'

'Am I? Does it show so clearly?'

'Yes.'

'How embarrassing,' he said after a pause. 'How corny. Anyway, you mustn't think that it's talking to you that gives me a sad look. Far from it. You've cheered me up already.'

'I can make myself look sad, too, if you want me to.'

'No. No. No.'

*

Some weeks later we became lovers. (Much to the disapproval of my brother, incidentally, for reasons I never quite understood. Perhaps he wanted to protect me from his friend. Also, being rather proud of the man's exoticism and waywardness, he probably wanted to protect him from me.) Everything started again. It was my first attachment since I had broken with Andy.

Shall I settle my accounts with Andy before going further? It seems appropriate to do so. Most of the time I knew him he was busy with a doctorate in Physics, and I was kept busy by my infatuation with his lofty, high-coloured, straight-nosed, glistening face. At the same time I did not know whether I despised him or feared him more. A mountaineer and a rugby-player, a member of the university parachuting club, a fanatic at the wheel of a car, he also went in for spontaneous dare-devil stunts – walking along the balustrade of a bridge, for example, or swimming too far out to sea. He did these things because they frightened him and he could not bear the thought of being afraid. Therefore he had to prove that he was not. But he did them also because he was a show-off and a melodramatist, who knew how anxious they made me feel and how easily they could reduce me to tears.

On the whole, though, he probably shed more tears than I did during our long-drawn-out affair. He was sentimental and weepy as well as reckless; each side of himself seemed to license the other. Since he took so many risks, I used to think he would not live long; he thought so too, and was always moved at the prospect of his early death. But it did not come to him.

After graduation I went to France, to Colmar, to work as an *assistante*; there I became involved with a married man, a journalist on the local paper. The news of this involvement brought Andy over hotfoot from Edinburgh. Angry scenes, all mixed up with a trip across the border to the Black Forest, followed: one on a footpath alongside the Neckar; another in the grounds of Heidelberg castle, with the tottering pink ruins looking on; the most violent, or at any rate the noisiest, at a camp-site in the forest. Tears running down his noble nose, threats of suicide muttering about in the bottom of his throat, as if of their own volition, Andy then went back to Scotland. After a brief interval I followed. Our reunion was not a success. It did not take long before he and I finally went our separate ways: he to the United States, me to London. He is today the head of a research institute in the United States; he is married and the father of three children.

*

Much earlier I said that I did not understand the people I was writing about. That includes me too. I know what happened to me, more or less; but even the best guesses I can make leave me ignorant of why it happened (is still happening); or why

186

I was the one who was chosen (who chose herself) for it to happen to.

It is as if we are all caught in an endless recession: I look back at this friend of mine, who looks back at Diana, who looks back at her husband, who looks back . . .

God knows what Foxborough looked back at. Or what he looked forward to. Annamaria? Being seen by me as an old, old man, in a raincoat, in Earls Court Square, a few years before his death?

*

My friend and I were together for about seven years in all – with some gaps and pauses and much longer, grateful resumptions. Holidays aside, we never actually cohabited for more than a few days at a time. Though we often talked of one of us moving into the flat of the other, we kept our separate 'establishments' to the end – he in Belsize Park, I in Clapham. (My move to Islington came much later, after his death and my mother's.) We kept our lives separate in other respects too. For instance, we would talk at length about what went on in our respective offices; I knew by hearsay all about his colleagues, and he knew all the virtues, vices, and idiosyncrasies of mine. But he rarely met my colleagues; and I seldom saw his. When office functions took place to which 'partners' were invited, we went alone. It was not that we were ashamed of each other; far from it; rather that that was how we preferred to conduct our lives. I was proud of my independence, or of the appearance of possessing it, and proud too that he did not try to interfere with it. Not in a manner which outsiders would ever have noticed, anyhow.

Occasionally he would tell me that I should be looking for 'another man'. That my 'best years' were going by fruitlessly. That I must surely want a husband and children as well as a career. That I would never get any of these as long as he was 'in the way'. To which I invariably answered that I, not he, was the best judge of what I really wanted. As far as I know he was faithful to me throughout; I lapsed into infidelity only once, on a business journey to exotic Manchester. (When I confessed this to him some time afterwards, I found myself

187

complaining that he was disappointingly, almost insultingly, undisturbed by it.)

Yes, he did 'perform' well enough, when the occasion arose. I was very proud of him for doing so. Proud of myself too. It was my skills that enabled him to do it. My passion. My admiration for him. The love I felt for him.

*

Looking back now I see two contradictory truths about some of the deepest feelings he roused in me. The one is that I always knew myself to be right for him, fated, the perfect match. I could say: his perfect victim. On the other hand it also seems to me that I was stupidly or wilfully slow in realising just how preoccupied he was and would always be with his memories of Diana – with the beginning of their relationship, with the forms it had taken while she was alive, and above all with its end, which for him (in one sense) was no end at all. When he first told me about his involvement with her I responded smartly enough with the tale of my relationship with Andy. Like an innocent, I wanted to believe that having exchanged his *quid* for my *quo* we were, in our different ways, trying to set ourselves free for one another.

But it did not work out like that. Obviously.

Well, not so 'obviously'. Not then, at any rate. It took time for me to become conscious of what was going on inside him, inside myself, and thus between the two of us. In the end or at the beginning I seemed to stumble into the truth without realising what I had done. How could I?

It happened like this. I was teasing him one day about how anomalous, even perverse, it was for an immigrant like himself to have had a spell in the Home Office, and then to start working so zealously for a right-wing, true-blue, conservative, English foundation. Should not that kind of thing, I asked, be left to the natives, to those who inherited the traditions of class and national identity and interest they claimed to uphold. 'Like Burke,' he asked ironically, 'the dispossessed Irishman? Like Disraeli, the converted Jew? Like T.S. Eliot, the *arriviste* American? They're the big three of English intellectual conservatism, aren't they? Can't you see, there's nothing like a being deprived of a past – or depriving yourself of one – to make you value it? To make you cling to it? People like me will invent a past, any old past, sooner than be without one. You wait and see. The more dislocation and confusion all over the place, the more people there are wandering about from country to country and from region to region, the more they'll fight for what they'll tell themselves is their past, distinctively theirs, theirs, theirs.'

He was silent for a moment; then went on, with a curiously begrudging movement of his head: 'Most émigré whites cleared out of South Africa because you couldn't be a liberal or a leftist there without virtually making a career out of it. I'm the exception. It didn't take me all that long, once I was here, to discover that I'd abandoned the place because it's quite impossible to be a *conservative* out there. What could you try to conserve in South Africa? Apartheid? God forbid.'

I said, 'You don't value the past. You're tormented by it. You just can't escape from it.'

'What do you mean?'

'I mean, South Africa.' Then I heard myself say, 'I mean, Diana.'

I had not known I was going to say her name. Nothing would have seemed further from my mind, a moment before.

He said stiffly, with a changed expression: 'That's not the kind of past I was talking about.'

'Nor me,' I apologised cravenly. 'I don't know what made me say it.'

But it was said. It could not be unsaid.

He was still looking at me curiously. 'She's dead. She's gone.'

'That makes it worse – for me, I mean, as well as for you.'

'You're jealous of her.'

'Yes, I am.'

He said: 'I can understand that.' He was unable to restrain himself: 'So you should be.'

Then he turned away; the conversation was over.

I cannot describe how I felt at that moment. It was something like despair and something like excitement, and each of these

189

leapt for its life on the other. I had done more than abolish a constraint between us. I had invited, I had positively incited, hitherto unadmitted feelings to take its place. Now that I was bereft of him, he was more mine than ever before. In myself, I saw him; in him, the one I might grow to become.

*

The result? This, ultimately. This task, which is coming towards its end now. Everything I have written here. The memorialising of a past which was his and not his; hers and not hers; which is now mine and not mine; which each of us has added to, made longer, been forced to live through and then beyond.

The truth is that I took over, so to speak, his memories of Diana and all they meant to him. I allowed myself to be haunted (as he had once been) by my fatal absence from the very scenes that had come to haunt me. A sense of displacement and vicariousness, of being a borrower from the experience of others rather than the true possessor of my own, became central to my life.

Perhaps that paradoxical condition is a more common one than I suppose. Perhaps it resembles what we feel every time we settle down to watch the news on television, say. Or, in a different vein, every time we read a novel or watch a movie. For me, anyway, it was both a slow and a swift process; an inexorable one, too, in both these aspects. Not surprisingly, the more I felt myself to be succumbing to it, the more fiercely I clung to my notional 'independence'.

Then we – I mean both of us – knew a kind of peace. We were able to enjoy the pleasures of our own intermittent, fierce connubialities.

The rest has followed.

*

Not as he is or ever has been (in all the forms
that dreams can take) but as the man he'll be
when decades still to come have come indeed
and gone again; knowing who he was and when
he was and how much time had passed between
the now of waking and the now he lived in
while he dreamed.

190

The room was sunlit,
empty, unornamented, painted grey,
a place for waiting. Back and forth he walked
as old men do – small step, long pause, and then
another step; bedecked in striped pyjamas,
as old men are, with slippers on his feet:
a sight too seedy-commonplace, he thought
(himself the viewer and the one he viewed),
for dreams or dread or even puzzlement.
His heart was full, but not with fear; there,
arrested, was the pang a man might feel
before he leaves the home he'll never see again.

Time to go! The passage booked!
                    With dreamlike ease
he also knew just how he'd make it. No food
would cross his lips until his weakness
became the strength – not his, not anyone's – of death.

The best came then. He turned to see her enter,
smiling indifferently, bare-armed, soft-necked,
and dreamlike ease gave way to dreamer's joy
at finding her at last as he had always wished:
an untried girl, a child whose life he loved
because it would be left behind. She'd done it!
She could never overtake him now . . .

                I trembled how to tell you –
                        *

I have no idea when it actively occurred to my friend that I
might (one day) be able to say on his behalf what he was
incapable of saying for himself. He never spoke of it, anyway.
It must always have remained a hope for him rather than a plan,
strictly speaking. Then the story of his relationship with Diana
would be saved from extinction; no less important, he would
get some sort of posthumous revenge on Foxborough.

   A slender chance, it must often have seemed. (Had he known
by how long Foxborough would outlive him he would surely

have despaired.) All he could do was to set me up for the job; and then rely on the difference in age between us. He told me much; he put down as much again on paper.

*

His critical biography of Foxborough had of course long since been abandoned. In fact, once the inquest was over the two of them never met again. My friend would never go to any function at which he thought there was a chance of the other being present.

Without telling him I was planning to do so, I did once go to a reading Foxborough gave from his work. I said nothing about it afterwards, either. The poet turned out to be frailer, greyer, more shortsighted, than the man who had been described to me; less commanding altogether. Perhaps it was merely (merely!) the effect of the years. He wore a dark suit which looked a bit too big for him; the top button of his shirt, above the knot of his nondescript tie, was undone. He put on old-fashioned, octagonal, rimless glasses before reading each poem and took them off again when he had finished; then he peered around the audience while he spoke, in a wavering voice, about the poem he was going to read next. With or without his glasses, I could not see in his eye the authority of which my friend had spoken. The first time he said 'I like this one' about a poem he was going to read, people made a noise of amusement; but they became embarrassed when he used the same phrase to introduce more and more of the poems. For the rest he prefaced them with bits of autobiography which did not always seem to be related to what followed, remarks about the verse-forms he had used, explanations of one or another allusion in the lines. Then came some renewed fumblings with the shafts of his spectacles, especially the pieces he had to fit over his ears, and flutterings among the pages in front of him.

His voice rang out strongly, it must be said, once he had actually begun each reading; it was noticeable also that when he had finished a poem he continued to stare attentively at the page in front of him, as if reluctant to leave it, and so to find himself marooned once again in the present, under the fluorescent lights of the bleakly collegiate room in Bloomsbury we were sitting in. ('We' being the usual desultory little gang. Some people collect cactuses; some examine steam engines; some go to poetry readings.) The poems meant little to me; I listened to him, not to them. Yet I was aware – how could I not be? – of the intimacies which they seemed to be offering to us and hiding from us. To this day I retain the memory of how he almost chanted his long lines, with their sudden clusters of consonants and occasional surreal images; of his juxtapositions of named, public events with obscurely private associations; above all, of the insistent 'I' who appeared again and again in the verse, always in different guises, some irritable, some clownish, some vatic.

It was strange to be there, to see him in front of me, after having heard him spoken about so much; stranger still to know that I was in possession of an utterly discreditable fact about him of which everyone else was ignorant. I wanted to say to the young, bejeaned, besweatered, handholding couple sitting next to me, the man with his hair much longer than the woman's – 'You see that harmless-looking old boy there? He wasn't always like that. He killed his wife. He let her drown. It was just luck, nothing else, that my lover didn't drown with her. That's the kind of man he is. Or was.'

Of course I said none of it. Perhaps it was then, sitting there, thinking such thoughts and saying nothing of them, that the matter was settled in my mind: yes, I would do what my friend wanted me to do, when circumstances at last permitted it. If that was the decision I came to, I certainly did not know it. All I knew was that, for reasons that had nothing to do with the hardness of the chair I was sitting on, I felt increasingly uncomfortable as the minutes went by. Finally, between one poem and the next, I got up and walked out. I was conscious of an old man's disappointed gaze fixed on the small of my back as I left.

The next time I saw him was in Earls Court Square, wandering about on his own, not long before his death.

TWENTY-ONE

So – having begun (more or less) with that image of a very aged Foxborough passing by me, alone in a London square, I thought that I would end with it too. All that remained was for me to say something about my friend's death, which took place so long before the poet's; then no more would need to be done. The work would be completed.

That is what I thought, until a few days ago. Since then I have been unable to write a word.

*

Let me try again. Try for all of it, this time.

Adrian Bester died at the age of forty-six, on the floor of Euston Station. Three ambulancemen were kneeling at his side. A small crowd of shoppers and commuters looked on while one of the attendants unsuccessfully applied a portable defibrillator to his chest. We have all passed by such scenes: limbs sprawled out on shining black-green marble slabs; brief-case and umbrella lying where they have fallen. There was no help that could be given him. At nearby University College Hospital he was pronounced dead on arrival. The cause of death was given as 'a massive coronary'. I was summoned there from my office shortly afterwards. My name had been entered into his diary, with home and office numbers attached, as 'next of kin'.

I suppose I was. I am still.

When they showed me the body, I seemed to see only his pallor at first; and then how deep his features were, each one of them. I have no other way of describing their appearance. It must have been the effect of their stillness. Not even in sleep had they ever looked so perfectly, finally, fully moulded to make him the person he was. The clamour of distraught incredulity which had accompanied me all the way to the hospital was finally crushed and silenced in my breast. No mistake had been made. It was him, no other.

*

But what sort of a person was he? I may not have understood him, all those years past, but I was sure I had known him. I had recognised him, to use one of his own terms. Now, as I sit here, I seem both to understand him better and to understand him less than ever before; and both states leave me at a loss. They also leave me wondering if I would ever have set out on this task if I had known at the beginning of it what I know now.

All I had to do, in order to turn my view of him upside down or inside out, was to carry out a little detective work, at this late stage, which I had previously thought to be unnecessary. Convinced that the essential facts were in my possession, I had never thought to look further. Still, moved by an unexpected impulse – perhaps because I was so nearly finished with the whole business – I went ahead; I called in some help, which I had scorned before. About a week ago I found someone who could translate into English the few passages in his notebooks which he had written in Afrikaans. Two or three days later she gave me her translations.

*

Apparently his native language had become a kind of half-code for him. It is hard to think of any other name to give it. He used it to conceal and reveal what he was unable to put down in any other form. It was as if he could not look nakedly at what he was nevertheless compelled to declare; or perhaps he could not bear the thought of others (me?) looking nakedly at it. But to say nothing, to admit to nothing, to leave unexpressed the truth as he remembered it and disclosed it nowhere else – no, that too was impossible for him. Hence the compromise he found. He reverted to the rejected, secret speech of his childhood.

There is something touching about his doing this. Touching, but also terrible.

*

What I have learned is that the story he told me about Diana's death was not the one he told in his notebooks. There, in his own hand, he makes it as plain as he can that if anyone abandoned

195

Diana on that beach, it was not Foxborough but himself. He could also be charged, just as he had charged Foxborough, of having done much worse than that.

If these entries are to be believed, he lied not only to the inquest but also (innumerable times) to me. He may also have lied, therefore, about the arrangements Diana had made with her husband before leaving the boat. The understanding between them may have been as clear and unequivocal as Foxborough and Annamaria had said it was. In that case Foxborough was not in the least to blame for Diana's death.

I do not know. I will never know.

The relevant passages are brief enough. They reveal, or purport to reveal, that he and Diana were indeed trapped together in that cove, probably as a result of their own inadvertence. (He blames Diana – whom he never names; he refers to her only as 'she' – for having let him sleep for so long.) These passages reveal too that in the moment of greatest danger he did not merely abandon her, he shoved her away, he hit out at her and knocked her down. He also says why he behaved in this way. Realising that they were cut off on that beach, he felt not so much fear, he says, as rage. To be trapped there, stuck with her to the very end, with her clinging to him, dragging him down, taking from him the one chance of escape he had – it filled him with a kind of fury he had never known before. The noise of his own rage, he says, was louder in his ears than anything the water and rocks could make. If he had to die there, then let him be alone when it happened, never with her!

Apparently he did help her up to the ledge, as she had wanted him to. But he was determined not to remain there with her. Once he had got her up there he shouted, 'I'm not staying here, I'm off.' She could not hear him, the tumult destroyed everything but itself. Yet she understood what he meant.

Another passage, standing by itself on a page, reads:

And to think I used to complain about not being able to remember her face. If only it would leave me now! She was crouching on the ledge, on all fours, with her head turned over her shoulder. I think of her now like someone waiting

196

for sex, but there was nothing of that in my mind then; only how much like an animal, a terrified animal, she looked. She was saying something, her lips were moving, but I could not hear what it was. I slithered down. It seemed as if all the roaring had suddenly turned into a hiss, and nothing else. Imagine all of it compressed into a hiss.

At least I was on my own. I didn't have anyone else to answer to. All that remained in me of them, of her and her bloody husband, was the terrible rage I still felt. It had the whole Atlantic behind it. And the rocks slavering, showing their teeth, going under, coming up once more for another bite, with the water running between them.

Again, turn over some pages, passing over this and that item written in English, and you find:

How far had I got? Nowhere! My back to the water, sidling along, clinging to whatever I could, too scared to look at what was coming at me; and there she was again. Of course she couldn't stay up there on her own, I couldn't blame her either, not even then. I thought only: 'You! Again!' Nothing else. We worked our way to the side. By then she'd lost heart, lost her head, lost everything. We were both half-drowned already, dragged this way and that. It never stopped coming at us. You needed both hands to hold on to those boulders. But all she could do was hold on to me, clutch me around the neck, scream at me not to leave her, never to leave her. I was also screaming. I tried to push her away from me and to pull myself away from her, wrestling with her fingers, twisting her arms, grabbing her by the hair. I even bit her. How she clung! So heavy too! And slippery! Then I hit her, on the forehead. Just once.

She let go, her head went back, she kind of swooped down, gone between some rocks. I looked for her, and then saw her again; swooping again, but upwards this time. I thought she was going right over my head, like a flying creature. But inert. Her hair stretched out before her. It looked black. Then she vanished. Later I thought I saw her again, but I don't know, it could have been a rock, water, nothing. By then I was thinking: 'I *can* do it.' I could see where to go. I would do it.

I still wonder, stupidly enough, as if it could make a difference now: did I actually knock her out?

So preoccupied had I always been with my disadvantages, destitution even, in comparison with everything she seemed to possess, I could never acknowledge it all the time we were together; but it was true, and it must be said. I was *her* fate.

*

There is just one other reference in that language of his – also on its own, in the middle of quite other matter – to the events of that day; or to its consequences, rather:

At the inquest he comes up to me. I'm still on crutches. He looks smaller than before. Everything looks diminished. From what he'd said to the papers I knew he didn't want to make trouble for me, or for himself, or for anyone else, living or dead. He says, 'Whatever happens here will make no difference to me. I'll always hold you responsible for her death. There is no excuse for you. You should be ashamed to be here. She'd be alive now if it wasn't for you.'

I said nothing. When I gave evidence he sat there staring at me. When he gave evidence I did the same to him. He wept suddenly, then went on. Afterwards he turned one way, with Terence at his side – also diminished, looking bewildered – and the rest of his gang. I avoided them. I went the other way.

*

The writer of those lines was just two years younger than his father had been at the time of his death. By abandoning Diana he had gained another ten years of life, more or less.

But she still had a longer life than he did. He never 'overtook' her, after all.

*

My turn next.

TWENTY-TWO

But not yet.

His papers have already been taken away by the garbage van of the Islington Borough Council. I saw them go; I saw the van rear up its end like an angry scorpion as it packed them into its interior, together with the rest of the multicoloured, malodorous refuse of a single week's living in a single Islington street.

Let him not think he is the only one who can strike out like a mad thing for his life! And let there be no regret and compunction about it, either.

I have taken everything I wanted out of those papers. Like a dutiful heir I have done what he wanted me to do; I have been through the whole story, and then through more of it perhaps than he bargained for.

Now it is time for me to abandon him, them, their past and mine. Now I can at last disentangle myself from him, I can pluck his fingers from my throat, shove and hit him away from me.

There is a PULL-DOWN MENU (so-called) on this machine which I can summon at any moment. It warns me that everything TRANSFERRED TO DISK will be wiped out irrevocably if I proceed to RE-FORMAT DISK.

The other offer it makes is more direct. It says simply: PRINT.

A NOTE ON THE AUTHOR

A South African by birth, Dan Jacobson has made his home in England
for many years. He is the author of several prizewinning novels and
many short stories. He also writes criticism and poetry. He is the
holder of a Chair in English at University College, London.